SNOW

SNOW

KENJI JASPER

VIBE STREET LIT
is a division of VIBE MEDIA GROUP, LLC.
215 Lexington Avenue
New York, NY 10016
Rob Kenner, Editorial Director
Theodore A. Hatwood, Jr., Director, VIBE Enterprises

KENSINGTON BOOKS are published by

Kensington Publishing Corp.
850 Third Avenue
New York, NY 10022

All Kensington titles, imprints and distributed lines are available at special quantity discounts for bulk purchases for sales promotion, premiums, fund-raising, educational or institutional use.

Special book excerpts or customized printings can also be created to fit specific needs. For details, write or phone the office of the Kensington Special Sales Manager: Kensington Publishing Corp., 850 Third Avenue, New York, NY 10022. Attn. Special Sales Department. Phone: 1-800-221-2647.

Kensington Books and the K logo Reg. U.S. Pat. & TM Off.

ISBN-13: 978-1-60183-001-2
ISBN-10: 1-60183-001-7

First Kensington Trade Paperback Printing: March 2007
10 9 8 7 6 5 4 3 2 1

Printed in the United States of America

For Butter,
without whom this never
would have been finished.

Acknowledgments

Maferefun Oludamare! Maferefun Yemoja!

This one is for all the dudes from the neighborhood who knew who they were and who I wasn't: Butchie, Rocky, Rick, Mani, both Damons, Rusty, Gary, and Marquis, whose life was taken trying to save one. Thanks to my parents and ancestors for keeping me on one side of the line, even though I knew the other so well.

Author's Note

Snow came to me in late 2001, not long after the release of my first novel, *Dark*, where he was introduced as a character. Like *Snow, Dark* was the story of a young man walking the line between the criminal life and a legit one. It was about a nineteen-year-old choosing between dark and light and the journey that brings about his decision.

This book is just the opposite. It's about those that choose the corners and dark apartments, the night instead of the sunshine. This was written long before there were more street books on shelves than anything else, back when my editor told me that something like this didn't have a place and that no one would be interested. Now that it's here, you be the judge.

—Kenji Jasper, July 2006

SNOW

I always liked the snow. When I was little I used to watch it come down from inside my living room. My eyes would watch joyfully as the flakes fell to the earth. My body would be wrapped in my *Return of the Jedi* comforter, 'cuz the heat in our apartment rarely worked and the warmth from the stove barely made it out of the kitchen.

That snow always seemed so peaceful as it took its gentle ride down from the heavens during those months with short days and nights that stretched forever. But that wasn't the reason I liked it.

I liked it because "Snow" was what people had called me since the third grade, back when Renee James said that the birthmark on my cheek looked like a flake of snow. I remembered the way she touched it with her baby-soft hand, and the way all the other girls in the class stared at that semi-freaky scene. Just then I was "The Man" in an eight-year-old's body.

But there were plenty of haters who didn't like my mark of greatness, the kind of boys who used to try to tear me down just because they didn't have any marks on their even-toned cheeks. Calvin Middleton was one of them. And I had to knock out one of his permanent front teeth for him to understand that hating wasn't tolerated on my watch. The entire school called him Snagglepuss for three whole years, even after his mama took him to the dentist to get it fixed.

But by the time I was fifteen, the word *snow* meant something completely different. It was the confetti made of cold that reminded me of how Black and broke I was, sitting on the rotting wood benches in front of the projects on 7th Street, selling rocks to the most desperate fiends just before dawn, just a few blocks away from the DC they show you on TV. I put rocks in the hands of people who trudged through the snow without a shoe in sight, livin' only for their next ten dollar hit.

Most of the time I'd be out there by myself. But sometimes my boy E, or my best friend, Thai, or Ray, who I used to do jobs with would be there to help me pass the time and make sure no shit jumped off. They'd ask each other if they thought they'd get out of school the next day because the temp was low enough for the powder to stick. It never mattered to me by then, because I'd stopped going to school.

My education came from the older boys who gave me lectures on the right way to do a hand to hand, from Lil' Will and all the times he told me to never try and shoot a pistol with one hand because of the kick. You should never rob anybody who was expecting it. Never kill, unless you have to. I learned how to keep my own blood from staining the soft white beneath my feet.

It ain't that I wanted to be selling death for cash. But I wanted to be free, free from all the jobs I watched my mama working, all the white faces that haunted her dreams with all the work they had for her to do for a check that never got us out of the projects. I didn't ever want to get up before the sun did. And I never ever wanted anybody tellin' me what I had to do. For all of that, the streets were the only thing that seemed to make sense. And by using all that I'd learned, by keeping my eyes open and my head clear as water, I'd actually made it to twenty-five.

But by then my boys had scattered in different directions, at least half on roads that led to the funeral home on 12th

Street. The other half got shipped out to Lorton and then to wherever the transfer told them to after they closed it down. Sooner than later all the faces you see are younger than yours. And they vanish twice as fast. You come home thinking about nothing but coming home the next night.

The ass in between don't really matter. You bust, and they read you the same script about commitments or what they want you to buy, meeting their mamas and all of that shit. But what I knew under the surface was that they didn't have what it took. Then I met Adele.

The way you look at the game changes when you end up with somebody. Your enemies become theirs. Your fuckups affect somebody else. You want to be more careful and take less chances. You hate that kiss on your cheek while you're sleeping because it means you won't see her again until later in the night. You just want to lie in her lap and let the world disappear. She knows who you are and where you've been, and she's cool with it.

"I'm not doing this on my own," she had said the morning she went back to work after maternity leave, as she slid a long black dress over her bra-and-pantied frame. Her stomach only sagged slightly from where an inflated womb had been not that long before.

"I know," I replied, as I did every time she said it.

Every job was becoming an odyssey, a journey through Hell and Heaven at the same time. As always, I was the man who didn't take shorts, someone who would put holes in any and everything that tried to keep me from making it back home for breakfast with the wife and kid.

Things changed even more the day my little girl got born and then again when Adele went back to work at her accounting firm after eight weeks of maternity leave. We had moved to a two-floor house off of U Street, close enough to what I'd always known but far away enough for her to not have to worry.

Kayi (which means "drifting snow" in Eskimo), my eight-month-old little princess, would let out these funny gurgling sounds on the mattress next to me while Adele got dressed, 'cuz she couldn't talk yet. But she always had a smile for her daddy. That little smile was all that I needed to get me through.

Yeah, every day belonged to my two ladies. But the nights were still mine. Senses and strength heightened beneath the silver moon that gave light to the DC skies. And when it came to a job, I always did what I needed to come out on top. On this night in particular, I needed to *acquire* a truck filled with DVDs on their way to the mall in Greenbelt.

Now, see, most people worked with partners. I always worked alone. My weapons of choice, two Sig nines I'd bought used from my boy Cuckoo, were tucked into the pockets of my bubble coat as I approached the loading dock of the old Woodies warehouse. Sigs are my favorite brand. Lighter than a Beretta, with the same clip capacity. And their sights are easier to align than Glocks. I monitored the three men's movements like I was the security camera.

Pac's "Ambitionz Az A Ridah" echoed from a box somewhere inside the warehouse as I filled my head with dreams of which movies I would take for myself before I handed the truck over to Jimmy to get my ten grand.

I moved so fast that they couldn't see me, and yet slow enough to seem like just another nigga walking by. I kept my hands in my coat pockets, fingers on the grips of pistols, #1 and #2, the black cashmere scarf Adele gave me for my birthday wrapped around my face to shield me from the late-night hawk and any potential police lineups. A nondescript skullie covered the rest of my freshly shaven dome.

I climbed the three steps that led to the loading dock, which stretched from one side of the building to the other, past several empty loading bays, all the way down to where the truck was parked. I hummed to myself as I moved along, knowing that one of the three men was gonna see me eventually.

It turned out to be the big man with the charcoal skin under his khaki work pants and matching bubble coat. He wore a blue ski hat with a white ball attached as he loaded what looked like his last two boxes into the truck.

"Hey, main man," I said in my friendly Mr. Rogers-type tone. #1 was flush against his left temple before he had the breath to answer. "Heard you got some movies for me."

I pulled #1 away from his skull, giving him the gift of a single breath. Then I smashed the butt of #2 into the dead-center of his face. His nose made a crunching sound as blood dribbled from both nostrils. He fell to his knees, whimpering like a wounded animal. A Tim boot to the back of the head put him flat on his face, begging all the while for me not to pull the trigger.

Another came my way. He wasn't turning my lights out either. I spun around and fired twice. The slugs went straight through both shoulders, splattering blood on the back of his coat as they came out the other side. He wilted to the ground, screaming the way broads do in the movies.

My final opponent, a short, skinny, light-skinned nigga with cornrows, was cowering behind the boxes in the back of the truck, hoping I wouldn't notice him, hoping I wasn't thorough, hoping I might leave him alone long enough for him to figure out an escape plan. No such luck. A boot just below the chin gave him the gift of flight, up and through the truck's unlocked back doors. He flattened on the dock next to the other two. The big man was still facedown and still murmuring to himself. Keys were in the ignition. I couldn't have written it better.

Three bitch-niggas. And they'd been dumb enough to leave the engine running. I shut the back doors, shifted into drive, and screeched off toward Florida Avenue, wondering why everybody didn't choose my line of work.

I never understood why Adele was with somebody like me, why it didn't bother her that I owned more guns than I did shoes, that I rarely got up before noon, that I paid for everything in cash. Every time I looked at her sculpted, sexy, slit-eyed face, it just didn't seem to fit.

She was the kind of woman who only looked right walking up in Georgetown, long legs sliding out of dresses that cost more than the tinted-windowed bucket I drove around Shaw looking for "job opportunities."

"Every job has risks," she had said, sitting opposite me on that first date, in a booth at the Market Inn, a plate of stuffed shrimp and glasses of white wine between us. She'd brought me there as a thank-you for the ride I'd given her. "I'm sure you do yours as well as I do mine."

She did a good job of acting like it didn't matter then, like she was one of those equal opportunity dating girls—you know, the ones who gave suit-and-tie guy from 16th Street the same shot as somebody like me. But she wasn't that. The real deal was that her daddy was nothing but an older version of me, hiring Black thugs to rob choice white cribs in one life and covering it up by robbing Black folks with the high-priced seafood restaurant he ran up on U Street. Her pops didn't spread the money around with her mom. All of that went to his *other* family, down in Southwest off of the wharf. That was one of the many reasons why I always went out of my way to give her everything she wanted.

I'd been driving the truck for a while when the sound of sirens flooded my ears. I had calmly cruised down Florida Ave, under the speed limit, heading toward the FedEx station where Jimmy was supposed to meet me. At first I was confident that they weren't after me. After all, I was only robbing niggas who were stealing. But when the flashing lights were in both side mirrors, I had to assume that something was wrong with the blueprint I'd drawn in my head.

Some variable on that dock hadn't been accounted for. More than likely the big man with the broken nose had played possum until it was time to call the cops. If he couldn't have the score, then nobody would. If I'd seen his ass again, he would've had a third nostril, in his forehead.

The sirens grew louder, but I stayed on chill. The problem with cops is that they're always so predictable. Everything is procedure and practice. Even their hunches are based upon patterns: if somebody does something one way once, chances are they'll do it the same way again. That's pretty effective for chasing those who treat crime as a way of life instead of just a means to an end. But I was a very different animal.

The only time I didn't wear gloves was when I touched my ladies. I never brought my own car to the scene of a score. I even dipped my bullets and guns in this chemical enzyme that made them resistant to fingerprints. Learned about it in a book I picked up about solvents right at my local library.

According to police procedure, one of the two cruisers would follow behind me as I popped the curb and entered the FedEx lot. Then the other cop car would come around in front to try and head me off. But those poor boys in blue forgot the laws of physics. Trucks can run through a lot of things that a car can't. They remembered only after their car was teetering on its side and I was on my way down the unnamed side street toward the underpass beneath the bridge that led to New York Avenue. I could hear more cops on the way.

I took out my cell phone, dialed a pager number, and hit pound. Jimmy could have what he was paying me to get, as long as he could get to it. But the approaching protect and servers were about to make that pretty impossible.

As I trudged through the mucky field of snow and frozen garbage, I wasn't upset that the night's main event had been stopped in the second round. The first thing I'd learned was that you didn't always get what you came for. The thing was to always get away, and clean. Sure, the cops were stupid and sloppy. But there were always more of them than there were of you.

My out came into focus about twenty yards ahead. My key to Escape City had worked perfectly. I tugged at the grating on the huge runoff pipe that eventually led to the southeast end of the McMillan Reservoir.

My boy Ray had told me about that pipe and how it connected to the sewer system. There was a passage that ran beneath the McMillan Reservoir to a service tunnel on the east side of Howard University. Over the years I learned the way, always in the winters, when the smell of sewage was not nearly as bad as it was during DC's insufferable summers. By the time I was twenty it was my own little secret lair. Those pipes and tunnels gave me the upper hand. I had all kinds of things stashed along the route, backup pieces and extra ammo, different fake IDs and emergency cash, all lodged in places the best sewer worker couldn't find.

The cold stung my face as my boots slipped and slid on the cesspools frozen solid by the season. I made my way down the slime-ridden paths, putting all my worries about Jimmy and the truck full of stolen DVDs as far behind me as possible. I had to find another way to deposit some cash into the safe in my basement. I never came back home empty-handed.

A lot of my ex-girls used to ask me why I didn't just get a regular job or go to college. They said I was too smart to be living the way I was. They said that I was driving fast on the road to nowhere. I always listened, because I always respected my women, but they were the same ones telling me about all the daily drama at work, about not getting promoted and bosses trying to feel on their asses in the elevators. They were the ones who married losers thinking they would win. They couldn't deal with my life. And I couldn't deal with the life they wanted for me.

Mike Mike was standing in front of the Giant Food on 7th Street, smoking a Newport and looking around for someone who probably wasn't going to show up. I didn't know what he was doing there, alone in a dark parking lot at two in the morning.

"Wassup, main man?" I asked him. We slapped hands.

"Just out here tryin' to get it," he replied, scanning the lot like a mall security guard.

"I hear you on dat," I said.

Mike was barely fourteen, young enough for me to remember when he was a baby, back when his sister Alexis had him in a stroller on the roof of her mama's apartment building. She said that she wanted him to watch us while we messed around up there. Alexis had always been a little off. But she gave me my first taste of what love was, of that weightless feeling you get talking on the phone with somebody all night until the sun comes up.

"Where's it goin' down at?" I asked, knowing he pretty much knew what I was there for.

"7F," he said. "But you ain't hear it from me, *main*."

11

"I don't even talk to God," I replied, already on my way toward the building where I grew into a man, preparing myself for what I hoped would be the final act in the night's play.

It was a poker game, a Wednesday night matchup that put local weed and weight money, high four-figure money, in the middle. It was the kind of game that went down just to show that the players had that kind of money to spend. No one knew about it except for the players themselves, a few crew members, and Mike Mike, whose job it was to stay in the parking lot and scan the building from afar, making sure that no strange cars parked or cruised past.

But they weren't expecting somebody like me to walk in on foot, say "Wassup" to the security guard I'd known for the whole time he'd worked there, and take the elevator up to the designated floor with enough bullets to change the neighborhood drug game in under twenty seconds. I didn't know the names of anyone up there, and I didn't care. The weight game never lasted. That was why I'd gotten out of it years before. When you stole, you got shot for what you did, not for who you were down with. I liked it better that way.

The elevator crept upward, stopping at almost every floor even though there wasn't a passenger in sight. The delay worked my nerves a bit. But I didn't let it rattle me too much. The doors opened on the seventh floor to an empty space that made me cautious.

I figured they'd have people posted outside, considering the kind of money that was in there. There should have been big men with big heat to discourage ideas like the one in my head. But most boys in the drug game were young, as I had been, and riding on the short-lived high that told them they would last forever.

I traveled the stretch of hallway like a ninja, listening for the loud sounds of young Black men with money to lose. It wasn't long before I heard them, behind the last door on the left, not 7F but 7H. Mike Mike had told just enough of a lie to cover his ass. And I had to keep loving him for that.

Standing in front of the door, I wasn't worried about what I was gonna say or how many people I was going to have to lay to an early rest. All I wanted was the money, so I could leave, make my final walk home, and sleep for the few hours I had left before breakfast. I wasn't preoccupied with inflicting pain. I didn't care about what the action would do for my reputation in the streets. It was just another job, just what I *had* to do in order to survive.

I kicked the door in the perfect spot and it crashed open, splintering the inside edge of the wooden frame. There were six of them that I could see. I didn't take note of their size or color, only their hands, several of which were already in laps and waistbands. That was a mistake.

#1 wounded one in the arm, another in the thigh, and a third through what sounded like his right lung. A bullet screamed by my ear and three more lodged in the doorframe just inches away from me. Too close. I darted into the hallway and rolled to the right, barely fast enough to evade the spray of bullets that punched through the outside wall.

Apparently they needed me to liven up the party. So I pulled out something special I'd snagged from my hiding place in the sewer tunnel to oblige them. I didn't have time for the OK Corral. I had a family to get back to.

I pitched the pipe bomb low and fast, aiming for it to hit the opposite wall so that it'd stop far away from the money on the table. I counted to four and covered my ears. It blew and I was back inside, gunning down everything that had the nerve to still be moving.

The glass in all of the windows had been blown out, and orange flame was quickly crawling across the dingy brown drapes, pushing clouds of smoke toward me. But I could still see my prize.

The money was all over the table, crisp twenties, fifties and hundreds. I salivated. But I was too fixated on the pie. That was my mistake.

A bullet exploded through my right shoulder. I couldn't believe it. I wasn't supposed to get hit. I let off in the direction the shot came from, even before I had the chance to see who it was. I twisted around to see blood gushing from her belly as she fell to her knees and then to the floor.

She couldn't have been more than seventeen, short and pretty with round hips and high cheekbones. She was the kind of girl I would have pulled back in high school, if I had ever gone. She dropped to the floor like a bag of bricks. That was unfortunate.

There was a shoulder bag on the back of one of the chairs at the table, and I went for it, tucking #2 back in my pocket to free a hand up. I broomed the money in and zipped it closed, knowing that the fire department would care about the fire before the cops bothered with the murders.

"I guess I won the hand," I said as I turned my back to the room of corpses. I was almost through the open door when I heard crying from the back room. Instinctively, I wondered Was it my baby?

No, it wasn't Kayi. But it was a kid nonetheless, something too undeveloped to move on its own. And through its ears, that kid became a living witness to my merciless mayhem. I thought about my smiling little Kayi and I almost dropped #1 on the ground. And I never dropped my heat.

I tucked the pistol away as I went to the back room and

put the crying child in her stroller. Then I rolled her out into the hall, away from the growing inferno. Doors would start opening soon, and I wasn't going to run the risk of being ID'd.

I took the back stairs down to the basement, where I crept out of the broken emergency exit that led to the alley in back of the building. As always, the night had kept things in my favor. I barely felt the cold, or the wind, or the profuse sweat on my brow as I trudged through the twelve snowy blocks that got me to our house. Adele's Acura was in the driveway, my '78 Buick Regal parked in front of it. I'd have to cut the treads off the boots and dump them, just in case.

I dropped my keys trying to get inside. My hands twitched more violently each time I struggled to pick them up off the ground. On the other side of the door I figured the shaking meant that I was coming down with something. So I made my way across the living room to the kitchen, where I gave light to the dark house. And then I put on the water for some tea.

#1 and #2 and the cash were on the couch in the other room when I hung my coat over one of the metal chairs surrounding the kitchen table. The pain in my shoulder worsened when I noticed the blood. The right side of my sweatshirt and the long johns underneath were soaked with the sticky redness. But I wasn't light-headed, so the blood loss couldn't have been too bad.

I got the paramedic's kit out from the bottom of the pantry and prepared to dress my own wound. Luckily the bullet had gone straight through. But I taped gauze on both ends so it would clot. I was finishing up when Kayi came alive upstairs, her cries as shrill as a soprano's. I raced up the two short flights to find the cause of her late night madness.

On the way I heard Adele snoring in our bedroom. It made me happy to know that I'd been there to answer our baby and to give Mommy a break after what had more than likely been a very long day at the office. The wound clotted on its own in the hours that followed, after I brought my sweetie down to the kitchen, got her a fresh bottle of pumped breastmilk from the fridge, and warmed it in a pan. My right arm was stained brown in places from the drying life fluid. But my baby didn't care. All she wanted was some time with her daddy, just like that little one back in 7H. I put *my* little girl down in her crib and put another strip of tape on my shoulder.

Sitting in the early morning darkness, I couldn't shake the image of that crying baby's mother and the hole that I'd blown in her. I tried to tell myself that she had been an obstacle in the way of keeping my two ladies in the style they were used to. I, we, needed it. Didn't we? I fell asleep on the couch, a folded-over towel underneath me so as not to ruin the three-thousand-dollar cream couch with any leakage from the wound.

Sun rays fell through the skylight and pulled my eyelids apart a few hours later. The smell of fresh coffee was strong in the living room air. Peering over the sofa back, I could see Adele nursing Kayi in the kitchen, a copy of the morning *Post* in her free hand.

"Rough night?" she asked me from what seemed like light years away.

"Tell me about it," I replied, my shoulder still throbbing with pain. I got myself up and walked over to my women with thick chunks of crust in my eyes. It should have been just another morning. But the words I used came from some unknown territory. I really needed her to hug me.

"I don't know if I can do this forever," I said to her. She looked up and locked her caramel eyes with mine and grinned like she knew something that I didn't.

"Nobody can," she said, pulling the three of us closer together. "Nobody can."

SIGHT

They say seeing is believing. Your eyes give your brain the full image, and the picture is worth at least two thousand words. Sight provides detail and perspective, color and dimension. It's the easiest sense to rely on. And I trusted in it fully on that night, in those last days in Southeast, days I would never forget.

The sky outside was dark gray with a blurry moon behind the clouds. Mama had been asleep for hours. Her grizzly bear snoring could be heard in both of the rooms that made up our apartment.

I didn't know why I was up. I didn't even remember rising from sleep, or the technique I'd used to slither out from under Mama's grip so that I could move into the next room. The one bed was all that we had.

But I made it my business to get to that window. Because my seven-year-old eyes wanted to see the big wet flakes falling into the thickening white blanket on the street below. My breath was just beginning to fog up on the cool glass when I heard it.

"Chk-Chk *Boom!!*" The noise exploded. The sound came from the hallway. I ran to the front door and fiddled with the broken lock just enough to get it open, something it usually took Mama at least a minute to do. But being me, I unhitched it in half that time and quickly poked my head into the icy air of the building hallway.

I looked to the left and saw nothing but closed doors and worn gray floor tiles. But to the right was the last thing I'd expected. Mr. Seasons's door was wide open and his feet were sticking out into the hallway. A pool of dark red blood was spreading under him. Vapors rose from the still-warm liquid into the frigid air. Mr. Seasons was wearing the Fila track suit he always put on after he came home from his security guard job at Anacostia High School. He was my favorite neighbor: a tall, slim, brown-skinned man who always let me come over to play Atari with him. Pac-Man, Pitfall, and Donkey Kong—Mr. Seasons had all the "like-that" games.

I already knew what death was when I ran over to his remains. I had seen it leave my building on stretchers, brought on by everything from cancer to twenty stab wounds from a two-dollar letter opener. But I had never been this close to it, especially not to a victim I actually knew. Little bumps rose on my arms, and I shook all over.

There were all these little holes in his chest, each point of entry filled to the brim with blood. I shook him and shook him, but he didn't budge. Something, however, did budge me.

A hand grabbed the back of my collar and flung me down the corridor. I was a paper airplane sailing through the air, until I thumped on the hard-ass tiles and fell into a tumbling roll that should have killed me.

Two men in black masks, shirts, and jeans stared at me from a few feet down the hallway. My head was pounding. I must have hit it somewhere along the way.

"You ain't see nuthin'," one of them yelled. His voice was almost a man's. He was taller than the second, silent one, the one holding Mr. Seasons's Atari game system under his arm, the two controllers flung over his narrow shoulder. The double cassette-deck radio that usually sat on top of the TV in Mr. Seasons's living room was in his other hand.

Just then I wished that I could've gotten there just a few minutes earlier. Maybe I could have done something to change Mr. Seasons's lack of a future. But as I got up, I knew I only had three choices. I could go back inside, wake up my mama, and let her handle it. I could go back inside and call the cops. Or I could go back inside, get under the covers, and keep the whole thing to myself. Any of those actions would have been expected for a seven-year-old boy with no weapon to speak of.

I noticed they weren't wearing coats, which meant they lived somewhere in the building. One of them turned to the other one, remembering something.

"Go get the piece, nigga! What, you was gonna leave that shit?" It took a moment or two for Taller to understand Shorter's words. Then Shorter grew impatient and finally darted back into the open door of the apartment, leaving Taller and me face-to-face, with only a few feet of hallway between us.

"I gave you a chance, lil' man," Taller said. Just then Shorter returned to the hallway with a black 12-gauge clutched in both hands. I didn't want to give them time to make the decision for me. So I ran back into the open door of our apartment as fast as I could. Then I shut the door, locked it, and listened. Echoes of laughter trailed down the hallway and then faded into a distant pattering of shoes on the outer stairwell. They weren't coming back.

I wanted to go back, though, to make sure that Mr. Seasons was dead. But my courage tank was on empty. I slid back under the covers next to my mama, who hadn't moved a muscle during the whole thing, and surprisingly fell back asleep ten minutes later.

* * *

"Thank you, Mr. Seasons," I always said when he would usher me into his apartment when I came home from school. "I wish I had a Atari at my house."

"Atari ain't nothin' in the scheme of things," he would say. "You got everything you need. You got a roof over your head, shoes on your feet, and a mama who loves you enough to keep you fed and clothed. And that's all you need."

He said those same four sentences every single time I thanked him. Yet they seemed sparkling new each time they left his lips. He pumped a vibrant hope through my little body. And now that hope had become as dead as he was.

I was a good boy back then, the kind who always said "please" and "thank you." I helped neighbors carry whatever groceries of theirs I could lift. I took the whole floor's garbage downstairs when the chute got backed up at the end of the week. I liked helping people. I liked the smiles I got because of it, the sense of relief in my mother's eyes from knowing that not everything in her life had been a struggle.

"It feels good to know I did one thing right," she would say on some nights, when she barely had the strength to sit on the couch and help me with my homework. Her body would sink into the puffy sofa cushions as she pulled me onto her lap, her arms pulling me against her breasts.

"I love you, Ma," I would reply. She would hold me even tighter after that. On some nights she even cried a little. On others my words might bring a smile to her almond-colored face or a tiny wrinkle to her little pug nose.

It was even better when I played clown and got her to laugh. With two jobs and her man long gone, there wasn't a lot left to laugh about.

I'd always suspected that Ma and Mr. Seasons had some-

24

thing going on. It was the only way to explain the half-hour trips he'd make over to our house while I was left alone in his living room to play Atari and watch channel 5. It would also have explained why he brought steak and ice cream over once a month so that we could "live it up a little." I liked him. And someone had killed him.

"You shoulda woke me up!" Ma yelled through her heavy sobs as too many tears ran down her face. The police had arrived around five in the morning, while I was out like a light, and filled Mama in on all of the painful particulars. She waited until I woke up to break the news to me.

I was too ashamed to look her in the eye as she told me what I already knew. So I focused on the center of the thick and lumpy oatmeal in front of me. I hadn't told her about what I'd seen. I just mentioned that the shot woke me up, that I'd gone over to the door and opened it to look out and see. She would've beaten me raw if she knew how far my curiosity had put me in harm's way, whether it had been for her man or not.

"I tried, but you didn't hear me," I said, playing the victim to the hilt. I was sure that in her heart she was glad she hadn't been there. She didn't want to see him dead and bloody in the middle of the hallway.

She put her index finger on my chin and forced my eyes to meet hers.

"If it's an emergency like that, you gotta try harder," she said, her voice increasingly clogged by the tears she couldn't hold back anymore. "Ain't no excuses for that."

She knew it wasn't my fault. It wasn't hers either. The only thing we could've done was gotten killed with him.

"Yeah, Mama," I said, nodding.

"You finish your homework last night?" she asked. The

tears then dried to a complete stop. She removed the remaining wetness with the corner of a patterned paper towel. Her eyes were still puffy, and I knew that she would cry again once I was gone.

"Yes, Mama," I replied. "I was finished before you got home."

"What you studyin' now?"

"Multiplying and parts of speech."

"So what's six times seven?" she asked proudly, knowing that I'd give her the right answer.

"Forty-two," I replied.

"What part of speech is 'pretty'?"

"Adjective."

"What about 'quickly'?"

"That's a adverb," I said with a proud smile. "You be givin' me easy ones."

"I *give* you easy ones," she said with a grin. "I'm not gonna stand for them kinda slip-ups when you in the third grade next year."

"I know, Mama," I said.

She looked at her watch, the same thin silver Seiko my Uncle Tommy had given her for Christmas just a few weeks before. "It's eight-fifteen," she said with a thoughtful smile. "Time for school."

I grabbed my coat, scarf, gloves, books, and lunch and trudged out the door into what was left of the snow blanket that had fallen the night before.

"You lucky they ain't shoot *you*," Keon said as he thumbed through the latest *Uncanny X-Men*. Wolverine and Sabertooth were on the cover, and I wished that I'd had the money to buy my own copy. "I woulda stayed in the house with the door and the chain locked."

"Man, it's messed up," I said back. "Mr. Seasons was real cool. I think he and Ma used to go together."

"Dag! For real? What you think they shot him for?"

"I don't know," I said reflectively. "It looked like they was robbin' his house. When they ran out, they had his double tape deck and the Atari."

"And that's all they took?" he asked, like a cop scribbling a burglary report. "They ain't take the TV or the VCR or none of that?"

"I don't know. I wasn't in there. But when they came out, all they had was the tape deck and the Atari."

"Then they was stupid," he said, bringing his eyes back to the picture of Wolverine slashing a Sentinel to pieces. "See, I woulda took everything." I scowled at the comment. He couldn't get away with stealing a pencil from someone else's box, much less a TV.

Keon was the only other boy on the playground who I hung with. I spent the rest of my time talking to the girls. Even back then they seemed to have more sense than any of us did.

"I think it was somebody from our buildin'," I said. "They didn't have no coats on, and it was freezin' out last night."

"Might be," Keon said as we lined up to go back inside. "But what you gonna do about it?"

In the background third- and fourth-grade boys broke sweats and skinned elbows in games of chicken and throwback football where the ball was nothing but a crumpled piece of paper. The bell rang and Keon and I ended our conversation as the on-duty teacher led us back into the building. Keon's words never left my mind. What was I going to do?

* * *

All the melting snow and slush made the ten blocks home seem like fifty. Every step of the trek was a different color on the grimy canvas of where I lived. Some kids my age from the projects on Sheridan Terrace were out in the middle of the street, coatless and throwing snowballs at one another. Todd and Edward gave me a nod as their eyes met mine in front of the Chinese carryout that always had the $2.99 crabstick special. In their early twenties, they were there every day after school, spending hours talking about nothing and trying to holler at every high-school girl that walked by.

"Girl, I gotta get you to the hospital!" Edward yelled toward a girl with French-braided hair who was barely older than I was, dressed in thick black tights and a leather skirt that hugged the curvature of her ass. She stopped for a brief moment to hear his punch line. "'Cuz your body is *sooo* sick!"

The slice of sexy rolled her eyes and kept walking, just as they'd expected her to do. Then they went back to talking, holding down that little corner like it was the last piece of concrete on earth.

Farther down the block I saw Ms. Barnes standing in front of the *Washington Informer* office, loading papers into the back of her Camry wagon so that she could fill all the bins in the neighborhood. "How are you doing today?" she asked. "How are you doing in school?"

"Three As and a B," I said, lying about the C I'd gotten in handwriting.

"Good for you," she replied. "Now make sure you keep up the good work."

She gave me a wave of the hand and closed her trunk as she moved toward the driver's side door to start the engine. Ms. Maybelle Bennett honked her horn at me just as I started past the McDonald's across the street from St. Elizabeth's Hospital, or the "looney bin" as Ma used to call it. The group of big red brick buildings was surrounded by high walls that had razor wire across the top. We never saw the folks behind those walls. And that was a good thing.

Ms. Bennett went to church with me and had a burgundy Chevette with a glossy spoiler on the back. If I ever got to make enough money, I would've bought a car like that for Ma in a heartbeat.

I turned the corner with only a block left in my journey. Then the seductive smell of fries hit my nostrils and I wished for the three dollars it took to walk away with a Happy Meal. But there was nothing in my pockets but two pencils, my keys, and a Garfield eraser. I'd have to settle for whatever was in the box back at home.

But there were some young men I had to deal with first.

"Hey, Pigeon!" Charles called to me. He called me "Pigeon" because he said I walked like one, with the way my neck brought my head back and forth a little as I moved. His boys, Ro, Dave, and Will, stood behind him, always surprised that I answered to the name so proudly.

To me it didn't matter much what they called me. For the longest time it had just been cool that they knew who I was. It made me happy to know that I was down with the big boys (meaning they had made it out of junior high). But the looks on their faces said that I wasn't so down just then.

"Wassup, Charles," I said. The weight of my backpack hung heavy on my small shoulders. He took a step toward me and then stooped down so that our eyes could read each other's.

"You heard about Danny, right?" Danny was Mr. Seasons's first name.

"Yeah," I said with a sigh. The growling in my stomach

wondered if the questions could have waited until I'd cracked the cupboards upstairs. "He used to let me play Atari at his house."

"People been sayin' you saw it happen," Will chimed in.

"What people?" I asked naively, not realizing that I was already tumbling into their trap. "Wasn't nobody up there but the people who shot him."

Will blushed with embarrassment that he had given himself away. Then Charles applied a vicious pluck to the side of my head, a pluck that hurt more than I thought it would. Fear spread through me like cancer.

"You a real smart kid," Charles said, just before he thrust his palms into my chest. My bag and I crashed into the staircase, and I rolled over twice before landing with a thud. Everything hurt, especially my head, still bruised from the night before. Hands grabbed both of my arms and lifted me to my feet.

"You lucky we ain't shoot yo' little ass last night," Will whispered, just before he rammed his fist into my grade school gut. I wanted to double over, but they held me up so I wouldn't bend. "You see where we comin' from, Pigeon?"

Of all the things to feel at that moment, pity was the first that came to mind. These punks wouldn't have lasted for a second against boys their own size. They'd even needed a weapon to take down Mr. Seasons. I wasn't scared of them, just the pain they were gonna make me feel if I told on them.

I hadn't even suspected Charles, even though I should have, with all the time he spent out on the corners, putting little bags in the hands of the people who paid him. And Will was always right out there with him. It seemed like the other two were in on it as well. The whole lot of them had probably just finished up a game of Pac-Man before they came out to meet me. I let out a heavy cough as they hit me again. My entire midsection hummed with pain.

"I wasn't gonna tell nobody," I blurted out. The hands let go of me at the same time, and I dropped to the ground, holding my stomach and wishing that they'd just leave me alone.

"Let's go back upstairs and play some more Pitfall," Dave said, probably just to taunt me.

It felt like an hour had passed before I finally got to my feet. Charlotte Marland and her little sister, Renee, were standing on the other side of the street looking at me like they couldn't have helped. The same went for the few grown folks who had walked right by me into our building. It was easy to hear about in church, but mercy was in short supply on the streets. I pulled myself up the stairs to our apartment and had a heaping bowl of Frosted Flakes and milk, the perfect fuel for the plan I came up with to get me and Mr. Seasons revenge.

I didn't know Landy Cunningham. But I knew his sister. Landy lived on the other end of my block in the house with the white siding and the tire swing in the back. He was barely seventeen, but he was already hooked into a little bit of everything around the way, from stealing cars to robbing the same five liquor stores to breaking into people's houses when they weren't home. If Landy wasn't doing it, he at least knew something about it. All I knew then was that Landy was Mr. Seasons's only nephew. And any good nephew would want to know who it was that murdered his uncle over some video games.

"What you want, lil' man?" Landy asked me as I took a

seat on the couch in his basement. We both had our black suits on from the funeral. Our ties were the same shade of blue. My shirt was white. His was darker, like a cream.

Everybody else was upstairs eating and mourning in Landy's ma's living room. The basement walls were plastered with pictures of Prince, Vanity, Sheila E., and Run-D.M.C. I didn't know anything about those singers back then, other than what they looked like. Ma didn't let me listen to that kind of music in her house.

"Your uncle used to live down the hall from me," I said, sucking down the last of the fruit punch in my clear plastic cup.

"Yeah, I know," he replied flippantly. "Him and your moms used to go together." I nodded, and his eyes met mine with a skeptical frown. "I hope your mama ain't send you down here to get no dough offa me."

A thought like that never would have crossed my mother's mind. It pissed me off to know that he thought she was that kind of woman. But I kept my head.

"I just wanna get the dudes that shot your uncle," I said innocently, though I couldn't wait to see what he would do once I told him.

"Yeah, so do I," he said as he rose from the couch and started to pace the room. "Them muthafuckas is gonna pay if I ever find 'em! And all they took was the damn Atari and a tape deck! Why the fuck you shoot a nigga for some dime-store shit like that?"

"I don't know," I said, letting silence hang in the air before I spoke again. "But I think I know who it was." I thought Landy would see a good beating as the perfect way to avenge his uncle's killers. And that was just what I wanted him to do.

"*Who?!*" he exploded. I didn't stutter or stall. Will

shouldn't have hit a little kid like me. They shouldn't have thrown me down the hallway like that. They shouldn't have called me Pigeon.

"Charles and Will," I said, flashing an evil grin. "They live over in my building." The look on his face said the names rang as loud as a school bell.

"You sure?" he asked cautiously. "I mean, how a little nigga like *you* know? You see they faces?"

"No, they had masks on. But they came up to me yesterday and beat me up and said they'd beat me worse if I told anybody it was them."

He let out a huff of disbelief, shaking his head uncontrollably. "Nah . . . nah, I *know* Charles. You just tryin' to get sumthin' started. What, they took your bike or sumthin'?"

I sighed. Why is it that folks never wanted to listen to the truth? "Landy, would I come down here and play games with you?" I said. "I ain't got no bike. I ain't got nuthin' they woulda wanted to take."

It didn't take long for him to figure out that I wasn't lying. I found out later that Charles was working for Landy as a scout. Landy gave him money to keep tabs on who had what in which apartments so that Landy could steal it. But in the case of Mr. Seasons, Charles had wanted the whole pie to himself: 128 bytes, two controllers, and five games. By snitching on Charles, I thought I'd only lit the fuse on a string of cheap firecrackers. But it turned out to be a box full of dynamite.

Landy picked up his cordless phone and dialed a number. Someone picked up on the other end, and he started shouting instructions like a gym teacher. A minute later he was ending the call and turning to me.

"You goin' wit' me, lil' nigga!" he yelled as he hung up the phone. Before I knew it, he had me by the wrist, dragging me toward the basement door and into the street. Ma was still crying her eyes out one floor above me, with the same untouched plate of chicken and potato salad on her lap. She was probably still waiting for me to come back with the punch I'd said I was getting.

Four other boys stood in front of Landy's house by the time he closed the door behind us. A tall dude with freckles and red hair was standing in front of the rest, holding a metal bat. No one else appeared to be armed.

Landy pulled at my wrist so hard that it felt like my hand might come off. His crew followed silently behind as the distance between his house and my building quickly dissolved.

Charlotte and Renee were across the street, jumping rope as usual. Ms. McDougal was bringing her regular cart of Wednesday groceries toward the building entrance. On any other day I might have offered to help her carry them in. All of a sudden, Landy stopped and looked at me again.

"I'ma ask you one last time," he said coldly, like a parent fed up with a child's tantrum. We were only a few yards away from the building by then. "Are you *sure?*"

I nodded. Doubts crawled through my head like roaches. What if I was wrong? Maybe I'd read too much into Charles's words. Landy jerked my wrist again, and the only thing I could think of was how sore my arm was going to be when it was all over. That was the last complete thought I had before it all descended into madness.

Charles, Will, and Co. were in their usual spot on the steps, rubbing their gloveless hands together to keep them warm in the icy cold. Their dress pants and shoes were visible beneath their coats, evidence that they'd had the nerve to make an appearance at the wake that morning. They were going to go to Hell for what they'd done.

Charles offered a perfect smile as Landy approached. But

that smile quickly faded when he saw me in tow. Ro and Dave both took steps away from the scene, knowing instinctively what was about to go down. Will stood fast, as if Landy and his boys didn't have what it took to make him move. Charles just didn't have the good sense to see what was coming.

Landy didn't say a word. Instead he plunged his hand into the breast pocket of his overcoat and came out with a black .45. He aimed at Charles's face, less than two feet away. Then he squeezed the trigger, supporting the gun with only one hand.

I turned and tried to run, but Landy tightened the grip on my wrist and yanked me back into position as he fired. His gun hand jerked wildly as the force of each shot flung his arm all over the place. That was what he got for pulling me so hard.

Ms. McDougal's tubby frame dropped to the ground in a faint. Charles hit the pavement, clutching his face as blood spilled through all ten fingers onto his clothes, eventually splashing its way onto the concrete steps beneath him. Will moved to help him, only to take a bullet straight through his throat in the process. He put hands to his neck as he dropped to his knees, choking violently as life left him as well. Landy put another bullet in each of them and let go of me, finally, to grip his wrist, which had already swollen to twice its normal size.

Landy's soldiers stood behind him, still ready to do his bidding. But Landy hadn't left a thing for them to do. Redhead approached and wrapped his arm around the executioner and led him back down the street in broad daylight with the others right behind. I stayed where I was, and they didn't try and move me.

I was both the cause and a witness to the scene that had

just been played out. Charlotte and Renee had their backs to me as they shook Ms. McDougal into consciousness. Ro and Dave were pressed against the building entrance doors, covering their eyes as they trembled with fear, still waiting for more bullets to come kill them too.

Will's blood continued to run down the stairs, reminding me of the water in the penny fountain at Iverson Mall. Charles had a breath or two left before his eyes froze dead. I'd seen three men die the week before I turned eight.

I had just wanted to make jokes about Charles and Will and their swole-up faces for a few afternoons. I wanted them to stop bullying me, to turn themselves in to the cops. But murder hadn't been a part of the plan.

The police showed up and asked me a lot of questions. And since I was a good kid, I answered them all, ratting out both the dead and the living because I thought it was the right thing to do. I didn't understand the streets yet. And I didn't understand that the cops never helped anybody but themselves.

Landy got a double murder pleaded down to manslaughter. He had a good lawyer. But that didn't stop him from putting the word out that he wanted me dead for snitching on him. I might have been the youngest potential hit in the history of the neighborhood. But Ma didn't keep me around long enough to give them the chance.

We packed up everything we could a day later, and Uncle Tommy drove us over to my grandma's in Northwest, to this neighborhood called Shaw. It was supposed to be a better place for me to grow up. But I had grown up too much already. I'd seen things in real life that Mama would've covered my eyes and ears for in the movies. And I couldn't make them go away, not even when I closed my eyes to go to sleep at night.

SOUND

"Stop!" yelled a female voice. She was so loud I was sure the whole 'hood could hear her. She was in danger, whoever she was. But Ma was always telling me to stay out of other people's business. "Trying to be a hero only got you into trouble," she'd say. And it was true, the last time I'd opened my big mouth, two people had gotten killed. The bottom line was that I should've known better.

I was eleven years old and full of myself, walking home down 7th Street after finishing my shift safety patrolling (yeah, I was one of those little muthafuckas with the orange belts that helped kids cross the street). I'd made that walk a million times since Ma and I had moved to Shaw, a neighborhood that seemed light years away from Southeast. In Shaw, the swings on the playground actually worked. The library had an encyclopedia set with no volumes missing. It was better all the way around, and according to Ma, this was the place where we were supposed to start over.

There wasn't a cloud in the sky that day. The April breeze spit sand in my eyes, blinding me for a second or two. For some reason, not a lot of kids were on the street, even though school had just let out. I shoulda known that something was up.

I tracked her screams to the rear of the old recreation center, or "the Rec" as it was known, a beat-down red brick building in the middle of Kennedy Playground. I turned the rear corner, heart racing, to the supposed rescue.

Chandra was the neighborhood fantasy, an eighth grader with the body of a chocolate-covered porn star. Her figure looked like an hourglass from no matter where you were standing. And she had a perfect-toothed smile to go with it. So it didn't surprise me when the high-school cats started to push up on her. Trying to rape her, however, was an entirely different story.

They'd pinned her arms to the brick wall with their hands, not far away from the gas and electric meters somebody had smashed to pieces years if not decades before. Her blouse had been torn open, revealing an off-white bra with fudge-colored cleavage spilling out into the wind. Her skirt had been pushed high above her waist and a hand covered her mouth while another held a pocketknife close to the taut skin around her throat. There were five boys surrounding her, the smallest of whom was at least twice my size.

It didn't take a genius to figure out what would happen if I didn't do anything. Still, on my own I was a sharpened pencil against a firing squad. So it was my heart and not my head that led me to bury my hardest fist into the back of the head of the boy closest to me. And it was my heart that brought my right hand to follow up my left as I began to pummel him from behind. A sharp jab to the back of his head buckled his knees. Then the other four were on me. And my heart was not enough to keep their heels and fists from grinding me into the asphalt. But at least I didn't get stabbed. Looking back, that was something I should've kept in mind.

As they went to work on me, I imagined that Chandra had used the diversion to escape, that she had run off just as the fists had begun to fly. And if she had, then all of the pain I felt was worth it, because I had saved her. And that would help me hold my head high as I limped home, whenever they finished bloodying me.

But when they brought it to a close with several falling elbows and a glob of spit flung against my cheek, she was still there. Blood trickled down from a cut above my left eye, and it hit me that Chandra was not interested in running from her attackers. Between that feeling and the full-throttle anguish from ribs that felt like they were broken, I wasn't sure if I would ever stand again.

She just watched me take my stomping like a man and then buttoned herself up, tugging her skirt back down to a presentable level. Chandra took the leader's hand and called him Shaka. I would learn later that this was a game she liked to play, that all the high-school boys around the way had to dig deep in their pockets to buy themselves a piece of this make-believe rape action. I had been trying to save a girl who was actually pulling the strings, who was having the time of her life only to have a bitch-ass sixth grader fuck it up for her.

Then the whole mob walked off, leaving me for dead, or as a bruised example of what happened when you got in the middle of other people's games. I only hoped that God would take me to Heaven so I could be with Jesus.

"You alright?" a voice asked me moments later. I cracked my eyes to see a kid about my age standing over me. I took the hand he offered, and he helped me up. He was acting like he knew me.

"Damn!" he said with a chuckle, surveying the damage. "They fucked you up good!"

"Yeah," I said, forcing the words over my bleeding lip. Ma would make me patch my own self up for being so stupid.

"I don't know why you tried to get in it," he added. "She'll do anything for that muthafucka."

"What? I mean . . . why?" I asked confusedly as we started away from the crime scene. "He ain't shit."

There were now all kinds of others sprinkled about on a street that I remembered being dead empty just a few minutes ago. Now they were starting back to their own business since I wasn't leaving in an ambulance.

I didn't really know the kid who was talking to me but I had seen him before. He was always over on the benches with the older boys, the ones who stood on that corner in front of my building 24/7. He was their main little man. And out of everybody around, out of everybody I'd met in the three years I'd been in the neighborhood, he was the only one to throw me a rope in a time of need, the Good Samaritan from Shaw.

"Shaka and them do that shit every once in a while," he continued casually. "Niggas chase her and catch her and start feelin' on her. Shit, sometimes one of 'em get to fuck."

"Why don't she tell 'em to stop?" I asked, far more concerned than I should've been.

"'Cuz she likes it," he said, shaking his head. "Girl is fucked in the head, but damn she got some nice titties."

My newfound friend was a lot heavier than me, with wide shoulders that looked like they could stop a linebacker. He had a huge, nappy 'fro and an Art Monk jersey with a pair of baggy Guess, the kind of clothes Ma never even came close to being able to afford to buy me.

"What's your name, man?" I asked.

"Ray," he replied with a grin. "But errybody call me Ray Ray."

"They call me Snow," I said, pointing to the birthmark on my cheek. He smiled.

"That's a alright name for a alright nigga. But see, what I'm thinkin' is you wanna get them niggas back. Least I would if I was you."

I saw his point. But I didn't want revenge. I deserved what I'd gotten, for being stupid, for sticking my head in someone else's business, even if my heart had been in the right place. Plus, I had a bad history with payback already. Making waves, any waves, was the wrong way to go. I'd learned that from the whole thing with Landy.

"Nah, they'll get theirs. And so will she," I said.

Ray Ray laughed a little.

"What's so funny?" I asked with a scowl.

"You think you Jesus or somethin'?" he asked.

"Nah, I just wanna do what's right," I said.

"Nah, man," Ray replied as we walked toward the benches in front of my building. "Around here you wanna always do what's right for you. He dug in his pocket and offered me a pack of Kleenex. You live up in here too?"

I nodded. "Sixth floor. But my ma don't let me out the house much."

"Oh, so that's why I ain't seen you. I'm on two. But we should hang out though, when you can. I'll show you the neighborhood."

"Alright," I said, feeling the ache from my ass-whuppin' again. I wiped the remaining blood from my face with crumpled tissue. "I'll see you around, then."

I saw him the next day, still hanging out with the hustlers on the benches in front of our building. Crack was brand spanking new, and anybody young with good eyes, hands, and nuts could make a lot of money real quick.

I went down there to shoot the breeze with Ray every once in a while. Then it became twice a week. And before I knew it, I was out there almost every day, just listening to them. And they listened to me. They said I was funny and smart, that I knew how to handle business. Their words went a long way to a kid with no friends and no father, nobody to show him how to be a man.

We never ran out of things to talk about down there. The conversations would shift from movies and TV to girls around the way. Their eyes would glow at the mention of BMWs and Benzes or how many parts they were going to get cut in their hair the next time they hit the barbershop. The words filled the time while they waited. Then they made a sale. Then they waited again. That was the business from sunup to sundown.

But the faces changed so quickly that I barely got a chance to get used to them. Some quit. Some got moved to other corners. Some died. Butchie had been the first one I remembered. After *New Jack City* came out, he got his box fade cut into a semi-mohawk like Nino Brown's. And he used to wave his cheap little clipped .25 around like it was a .44 Magnum. He got popped one morning just before sunrise, waving that gun around while the stick-up kid pulled the trigger on his.

Butchie had gotten the corner after Alonzo. Then after Butchie came Archie. Then the raids started. Mayor Barry had put together a task force before he left office. When the smoked cleared, Troy was the last man standing, having beaten both the bullets and the boys in blue. And claiming victory over both, he ran six whole blocks from the very corner where it had all started on O Street all the way up to the library.

"I don't wanna see you down there again," Ma threatened when my mostly As began to be sprinkled with Bs. "You understand?"

She didn't have to lecture me. I knew that what they did

out there was wrong. I saw the films and videos in school about what drugs did to people. And I saw all the boys who had died over who controlled the business that tore people apart. But my main man Ray was in the middle of it. And he had a different view of it all than Ma and I did, one which he took the time to share with me at every opportunity.

"They ain't got no choice," he said of the hustlers we knew. "Some of 'em got babies on the way, or don't nobody work in their family. You can't make no real money sellin' shoes for five dollars an hour at Kinney's."

I knew he was full of shit from the beginning. But hearing him say the words over and over again somehow got them to make sense to my young, impressionable mind. Ray had been the only dude who was there for me when I had needed a hand. That made his opinion matter more than anyone else's.

"Yes, Ma," I said, knowing for the first time in my life that I wasn't going to obey her. I had found another family down on the street. And I couldn't just leave them, not at thirteen, when everything was just getting started.

I still went to school every day, for Ma's sake. And I changed those Bs into As through the rest of junior high. Once that happened, Ma didn't seem to care where I went, as long as things were on the up and up on paper. Then the worst thing that could've happened happened. My grandma came down with chronic pneumonia. And Ma had to go down to Richmond to take care of her.

What was supposed to have been a week or two turned into four months. Grandma fought the Reaper every step of the way, and someone had to be there for her. Grandma gave Ma the money for the rent, and my cousin Derrick moved into the house to keep an eye on me.

Derrick, of course, couldn't take care of what he didn't see. At twenty he was so concerned with peeling tenth graders out of their panties that he turned a blind eye to my regular disappearing act. I made sure to show up at five-thirty and ten PM, when Ma always called, as regular as clockwork. Soon as I said good-bye, I was back down on the corner.

My day of reckoning came just a few weeks before Ma's return, on a Thursday in the middle of May, when everybody was outside because the air-conditioning in our building never worked. By then Troy held the longest record for slinging on 7th Street. I considered it an honor that he asked me to do him a two-hundred-dollar favor.

I had seen Ray do those kinds of favors all the time. The profits kept him in Guess and Fila and Madness Connection without even having to break a sweat. But being who I was and coming from where I came, I needed a hand to push me in or pull me away. And with Ma gone and the spring air so warm, I let the streets pull me further and further away from who I'd been.

"It's way too dangerous," I argued after Troy offered me the job. "What if the jump-outs see me? I ain't tryin' to go to Oakhill. The money ain't worth that much."

"Don't be a lil' bitch," Ray said, taunting me, knowing just the way to get me (or any boy my age, for that matter).

"All you gotta do is use your legs and your eyes," he continued. "You see the jump-outs, you drop the bag and run 'til you can't no more. If not, you go in the buildin', drop the shit off, come back, and get your money."

Not everybody was trusted with making runs. To be down with Troy, he had to know where you lived and who you were cool with, where you went to school, everything the game ultimately required you to give up. He had to know you were a true soldier before he sent you out to war.

"You a fuckin' Green Beret in my book," Troy said as he made me the offer. "But I only want you to do it if you really wanna do it."

I didn't care about clothes or chains or cars. I just knew that Ma was going to need money when she came back. A lot of people were out of work in the city as it was, and Woodies would probably say that she'd been gone too long to let her come back to the juniors department. If I just made one run, there'd at least be a little something that I could stash away and say I'd saved it up washing cars or collecting cans—something cute and reasonable a mother would be willing to believe. Then she wouldn't have to worry as much. And she could sleep later. I told myself that that would matter more than what I'd done to get the money.

I didn't look in the Giant Food shopping bag when the time came. I knew what I was carrying as I walked into that house with the yellow siding on 6th Street. The acoustics on the stairwell gave my breathing an echo as I climbed three floors to my destination. I knocked three times on the scratched wood door. It cracked open soon after.

Troy's cousin Cameron peeked down at me, making the opening just wide enough to grab the bag and snatch it inside. He shut the door to preview the merchandise, opened it again, and then placed several folded bills in my open palm. I stuffed them in my front pocket, and, with a sigh of relief, headed back to the corner to collect my cut of the paper.

Ray was right. It had been easy. So easy that it wouldn't hurt to do it one more time, or one more time after that. For our customers, smoking was the addiction. But it was the running that had me hooked. It reminded me of when I was little, and all the people I'd met in my building by helping them out. The members of Shaw's shady side smiled when they saw me coming. And their teeth usually looked the same as anyone else's.

The knot I was hiding for Ma turned into two. Any excuse I could make up wouldn't cover it. So I had to do some spending: a few shirts and pants, sneakers and some sweatsuits, even a few gold chains for special occasions. They were merely accessories that went along with the job. By the time she came back, Ma knew just by looking at me that too much of what she'd taught me had been washed away like houses in a flood.

I tried to teach Ray how to stack his money the way I did, to save it up so if we had to stop we wouldn't be broke again and the family bills would still be paid. By the time I was fifteen, everybody on the block knew me as "Lil' Snow." And by sixteen, Lil' Snow had a brand new '92 black Maxima with the dark tints and the matching headlight covers.

Through those years, Chandra had always stayed in my mind: the curves in her thighs, those dick-suck lips, and titties that had only gotten bigger with time. I'd seen her going to and from school with Shaka and with others, and sometimes by herself. She'd picked up a little weight, but I could barely tell. There were so many things that I'd wanted to say to her, questions I wanted to ask about that day long ago. But I didn't, and eventually they all churned into a kind of hatred for her, a feeling of disgust laced with the love that had inspired me to try and save her in the first place.

I needed to know what those other dudes had that I didn't. I had some money and a nice ride. Why wasn't she knocking on my door? I was at my height. And she was supposed to recognize that.

There was only one thing to do when she finally approached me one afternoon in the winter of '91. I was parked up by the CVS on Georgia Ave, waiting for Ray to come out of this girl's house, when she came strolling up in a leather skirt so tight that I couldn't figure out how in the hell she managed to walk.

"Is that yours, Snow?" she asked as I leaned against my car. She knew it was. But she wanted to play the game. And I was with it. I took her upstairs to my mother's apartment and cashed in my prize, doing my best to show her that I had everything that Shaka had, that I was just as much of a contender as he was.

It was almost like her tits defied gravity when they came out of that black bra, the nipples as hard and straight as soldiers. I remember the way she moaned when I put my fingers inside her and the way she begged me to fuck her when I sloppily played with her clit. And I remember the way she looked up at me when I came in her mouth, like I was a god she was blessed to suck dry. After that I had her, or at least I thought I did. All I could do was laugh out loud when she casually mentioned that she was having Shaka's baby.

"Broads is only there to keep your dick in shape," Ray had told me once. I didn't believe that, though. But maybe the ones I wanted just weren't the ones for me, especially after they found out how I got the ride they loved to cruise around in. And that was just a small part of a much bigger problem.

"I can see it behind your eyes," Ma said on one of the few nights we sat at the table and had dinner together. "It's eating away at you."

I remember laughing after she said it. But neither of us thought it was funny. She was right. Something was nibbling away at me from the inside out. I felt it thickening as its strength increased. It was a dark, cold, and disagreeable thing, something that made the old Snow, the wannabe hero, want to run and hide.

* * *

The Cisco had been too much for me when Lana, Ray's sister, had a birthday party at their mom's apartment. The whole neighborhood was there, so many girls with so much ass that my dick got sore just from looking. But I didn't really want them that night. As I sipped my drink it hit me: I still wanted Chandra.

Shaka was in the kitchen handcuffing her like a cop. I stared at her plump ass pressing against the grease-stained wall next to the trash can turned makeshift punch bowl. I hated him. He was almost nineteen and still fucking a girl my age. And of course I hadn't forgotten about him beating my ass to a pulp. Those things, added to the liquor floating at the top of the mix, pried my mouth into the "open" position.

"Hey, Shaka!" I yelled across the overcrowded room.

He looked up in a flash, and his eyes met mine. He wore those same brown Guess every weekend, as if people weren't going to notice.

"You a real bitch-ass muthafucka!" I announced. I had a .38 in my waistband if he wanted to get cute and a good right hook if he wanted to be a man about it.

"What you say, nigga?!" he yelled, letting go of Chandra's wrist as he charged toward me. His boys fell in behind him. I counted three, which was perfect. Ray, E, and my best friend, Thai, were to my left and right before they could even get close. And we destroyed them.

I came down on Shaka with everything I had. Every fist was knuckled with the hate I'd held back for so long. And that hate wasn't just for me. It was for the money and toys he'd taken from the little kids in my building in the years after that day at the Rec, for taking my boy Scoonie's Jordans at knifepoint and then breaking his jaw because they didn't fit. It was for Chandra, and for him beating the shit out of me just because I'd tried to be a hero back when Shaw really could have used one.

I don't think him and his boys ever got a single punch off. We came down on them like thunder and lightning. I felt it when my heel snapped one of Shaka's ribs. I could see someone's eye swelling closed. There was somebody's blood on Thai's pant leg. Ray pulled a dude's arm so hard that he dislocated it from the socket, making his victim scream like a bitch in a horror movie while the rest of the party looked on.

When it was over, we dragged them all out of the place by their ankles and necks, into the hallway. The rest of the party went back to having a good time while we rolled them like tires down the emergency stairwell, where there was no re-entry into the building. And that was the last we saw of them that night.

By the next afternoon, the whole neighborhood knew about what had happened. And they were all on the corner the next day to hear my version of it. Thai and E were in school, but Ray was there with me. And we all laughed and played while the rookies did the business. We were so stuck on ourselves we didn't notice Shaka and company rolling up on the other side of the street, their blackberry faces so bruised it would have been easy to mistake them for somebody else. But a chill rushed through me that said something was about to happen. I managed to pull Ray to the ground just before they opened fire.

But Ray jumped right back up with his .45 in a firm grip and fired back across the street like bullets didn't faze him. The three gunmen scattered, firing blindly into the wide-open space of 7th Street in broad daylight. Ray took one dead center in the abdomen. Another hit Troy's little brother,

Arty, who just happened to be turning the block on his bike when the whole thing jumped off.

The clicks of empty chambers sent Shaka and his boys on a race toward the playground, where they took cover behind the Rec, the same place where he and I had begun our feud four years earlier.

Ray was already facedown on the pavement, convulsing from shock. A pool of blood had formed beneath him. Troy rushed to the aid of Arty, who was crying like an infant from a wound through his leg. I knew what I had said and done. It was only right that I be the one that got hit. But instead they'd put down Ray, my man ninety grand. And with only a split second to think, I decided that I couldn't let him die unavenged.

I got to my feet with my .38 in a tight grip, the first piece I'd ever owned, and slunk toward the Rec like I was Shaft. I'd never pulled the gun out before, not even to point it at myself in the mirror, *Taxi Driver*-style. But in the heat of my rage it was the only tool for the job. They were behind that building, reloading. And I wouldn't give them the chance to hit anybody else. Ever.

I turned the rear corner of the building like a cyclone, the gun gripped in both hands. I fired like a marksman even though I'd never done it before and put holes in every skull or heart I saw there, dead center. Shaka got two. Blood stained the brick and the concrete and my brand-new pair of Girbauds. I stood there for a moment, just to catch my breath, then spun around and raced back to the corner to see if my main man was still alive. Lana was there by the time I got back, leaning over Ray on her knees with tears in her eyes. But he was still breathing, muttering something unintelligible with his eyes closed. He'd live. I just had to make sure that the rest of his life, and Troy's, and mine, wasn't spent in anybody's lockup. It wouldn't be long before we heard sirens. The cops kept two cruisers over at Dunbar, which was only a few blocks away.

Lana and I quickly gathered every piece from our corner and put them into the tote bag she happened to be carrying and then took the bag into her building and down several stairwells to the basement. When the paramedics arrived, I was emptying the rounds and tossing the shells and pistols into the bottom of the furnace along with my bloody clothes.

I'd read a few books about police procedure back when I first started hustling, about fingerprints, gunpowder residue, and nitrous tests, about evidence and due process. I'd even checked out a few police academy textbooks. I wanted to know everything they knew, so that I could make my own rulebook, one that would juke them every time.

I was going to get away clean. But still, something was wrong. As I stood there, in the bowels of the building I called home, getting away wasn't what concerned me. What really bothered me was that I wasn't scared, not in the least.

Some kind of guilt should have hung heavy on my slim shoulders. But they were as light as air. I felt nothing, aside from my worry about the wounded man who had brought me into the game. That something, that something that was nibbling away from the inside, had found a hole to the surface. And there was a part of me jumping for joy that it had finally arrived.

CELL

Everybody gets caught. The trick is to not let it happen too often. I only let it happen once. And even that one time, it wasn't my fault. The jump-outs had raided our corner on a day I wasn't even out there. I had been heading up 7th on the way to the corner store with $300 in my pocket to get some green apple Now and Laters, my favorite candy in the world, and they just ran up on me with the bracelets.

They threw me into the back of a blue and white with Troy and Ray. Both seemed just a little too happy that I was going down with them. Crabs in a barrel, man. That shit don't ever change.

"What's your full name?" the gray-haired dude with the badge and the tight polyester asked me in booking, just after they'd unhooked the daisy chain of cuffs that bound us all together. They'd seized the three yards in my pocket and my pager and read me my rights. But I still didn't know what I'd been charged with.

I was seventeen, less than a hair away from adulthood and the time that comes with it. My veins throbbed. My breathing heavied. Jail had suddenly become like church in my mama's house. There was no way I could talk myself out of it.

The holding area was packed tight with faces similar to my own: young, tense, and trying not to show either. A fight broke out between two dudes, one from 640 and the other from Ivy City, two neighborhoods that somehow ended up rivals even though they didn't have much to do with each other. But it didn't last too long. The one with the nappy Afro took an index finger in the eye, and a barefoot stomping followed soon after. I quickly understood why they didn't let us keep our shoes.

Things were back to normal by the time the guards got there. Afroman had crawled into a corner, holding his knees to his chest in hopes of healing quicker.

Ray and Troy chatted it up like they were in a high school cafeteria, slapping hands with familiar faces and shooting the shit as if there wasn't a judge to see in the morning. I had things to do, TV shows to watch, a copy of The *Art of War* to get back to the library around my way. And I was afraid, more afraid than I'd been in my entire life.

I mean, I didn't look it. There was no trembling or glancing around like I was nervous. But that icy feeling slithered from my scalp to my toes and back up again. I'd never been in a cage before, had never been in a place I couldn't leave, other than my mama's house.

Up until then, the game hadn't seemed any different than working at the mall or delivering newspapers. Like any job it had its rules and risks. Those poorly dressed men in unmarked cars had been our only distant threat. But they'd finally come out of their cruisers for us, and on the one day we least expected it, a day when I wasn't even out there.

"What the fuck are we gonna do," I said, not particularly to anyone. Several heads turned in my direction. I'd apparently shown too many cards far too soon.

"You need to relax, nigga," Troy said. "They ain't got shit on you. No weight. No gun. You'll be outta here in the mornin'. See, me and Ray got bigger problems."

"What you mean?" I asked.

"We been in here before," Ray blurted before Troy could get the words out. "They let us off with warnin's, gave us community service, picking up leaves and trash, all that shit. They 'bout to hit us with some real shit this time."

I remembered those days here and there when I had to work without them. I was so nervous on my own that I moved the corner to the tiny park on Kennedy Playground, where I sat in the shade and took care of the customers, all the while thinking of my boys and what had happened to them after the jump-outs put them in the backs of three separate police cruisers with three separate sets of cops in the front seats. I had sworn that that was never gonna be me. Now that arrogant feeling that I was above ever getting caught was melting faster than dropped ice cream.

"What you mean, 'real shit'?" I asked them. Troy grinned as he placed a hand on my shoulder.

"You scared, huh?" Troy asked nonchalantly. I made the stiffest face I could and held it until the muscles in my cheeks began to ache.

"I'll take that as a yes," he smiled. "But let me put it to you this way: this shit is a birthday party compared to the way they do things over at the Tank."

The Tank was the main DC jail, the clay-bricked compound next to DC General where they kept you until trial, sentencing, or transfer. In there it didn't matter what kind of heat you'd carried or what corner you held. In there, you had to make a name for yourself all over again.

I liked the rep I already had as a free man out in the streets of Shaw. But as the minutes burned like hours, I was willing to trade it all in—the car, the clothes, the cash, and even the name—just to breathe free air outside of the precinct.

Another fight jumped off an hour later, and we were in it. It had something to do with Ray's jeans or my shirt. I ended up ramming some fat nigga's head against iron bars until it bled. Ray had his opponent on the floor holding his jaw. It was somewhere around then that two guards snatched me out.

"Just in time," the freckled one with red hair said. "Somebody's here to see you."

They brought me out in cuffs, wrists and ankles, just to let Ma see how much of a criminal I looked like as they sat me down next to her on a hard wood bench in open view of everything the station had to offer. My joints ached almost immediately from the restraints.

"They hurt you in there?" she asked. She wore the fuchsia-colored sundress I'd bought her for her thirty-sixth birthday.

"Nah," I said, looking her in the face only to absorb the shame her stare filled me with.

"Lana called me at work," she said, wiping the summer sweat from her brow. "I came as soon as I could." She brought her soft hand to my cheek, aggravating the fresh bruises that had just formed there from the fight.

"Thanks, Ma—"

"Don't thank me for anything!" she exploded. "I ain't come here to get you out!" Heads turned, and a few nosy officers cracked smiles at my humiliation. Then she continued.

"Andre (yeah, that's what my mama named me), I came here because you're my only boy. I came here because as your mother there are things I had to tell you now. Maybe I shouldn'ta gone to Richmond. But I'm my mother's only daughter. And at the time, I thought leavin' you with Derrick was best. I didn't wanna take you outta school or take you away from your home again. I promised myself I wouldn't do that again after the last time when you were little. But I don't know what's happened to you! You used to be such a good boy. I'm not sure what it was that made you change."

Somebody else might have jumped in to argue. They might have screamed that they'd been picked up by mistake, that they were walking down the street minding their own business when the police grabbed them and shoved them into the back of a cruiser. They would've said whatever it took for their mothers to believe that they were still good.

I knew better. And I respected Ma too much to try to play her for a fool. We both knew that I was bad. And I wasn't sure if I'd ever be good again. And my mother still wasn't finished.

"I tried to turn a blind eye at first," she continued. "I told you not to be down there with them boys on the corner no more. But I also knew a boy shouldn't grow up alone, not the way you did. You needed a father, brothers, at least an uncle. But I didn't have none of that to give you. I did the best I could."

I kept my eyes on hers, but I still couldn't help but notice all the police and prisoners gazing at us from the periphery. This wasn't the place where you wanted to have a heart-to-heart with your mother. It wasn't a place where we ever should have had to talk, period.

"So what happens now, Ma?" I asked, sounding like the good boy I used to be. She flashed a quick smile.

"I don't know," she said matter-of-factly. "But you can tell me when you get outta here." Then she started to her feet.

"What you mean?" I asked, confused.

"It's about time you see the other side of things, see what I was tryin' to protect you from, the things your daddy—"

I had to cut her off. She couldn't just leave me there. "You not gonna get me—"

"I can't save you, son," she interrupted. "Best thing I can do is let you go and hope that some kinda way you'll find what you need. Then you can come back to me. I'll pray for you every night until that happens."

"You kickin' me out?"

"You kicked yourself out, son," she replied, sounding as if she'd lost a war. "I'll leave your clothes and things with Ray's sister. She and I already talked about it."

I didn't know what to say as I watched her start toward the exit. I couldn't remember a time in my seventeen years when she hadn't been there when I needed her. Now that was all over. If I'd only had the foresight to understand how what I'd been doing affected her, how I had put her at risk without meaning to, how I'd been blind to it all until it was too late.

She had seen it in my eyes before anyone else had. And now she'd thrown in the towel after too much trying. My eyes followed her form into the daylight beyond the precinct lobby. That was the last time I saw her for a long time.

Redhead uncuffed me twenty minutes later. The charcoal in his tie matched his slacks. He leaned toward me, his gun in grabbing range if I had a death wish. But I'd already been disowned. And that was as close to death as I was ready to come at that juncture.

"You don't remember me, do you?" he asked. I drew a blank. "But that's alright. You was little then anyway. I used to live on your block, over off of MLK."

The memory snapped in like a piece of Lego. He had been the one with the bat that day Landy had turned the front of my building into a bloodbath.

"Yeah, I remember," I said and yawned, pretending not to care. "How the fuck they let you be a cop?"

"'Cause I didn't pull the trigger," he said with a solemn smile. "Landy did."

"Whatever happened to him anyway?" I asked, barely even remembering what the boy had looked like. It was his .45 with the scratched barrel that had been eternally etched into my brain.

"Last I heard he caught another case. Ain't seen the light of day yet. But I haven't talked to him in years, not since I joined the force."

"So why you remember me?" I asked, trying to seem like I didn't want him to keep talking, as if he wasn't helping me to avoid the pain and uncertainty that were already coursing through me.

"How could I *not*?" He grinned as he took a seat on the bench next to me. "Hoped I wouldn't see you here, though."

"Hey," I said, shrugging my shoulders, trying to be arrogant. "It is what it is."

"You ain't so far in that you can't turn around," he reminded me. "I used to see you, even if you didn't see me. Everybody used to say how smart you were, that you were a good kid."

He stopped for a moment to search my eyes for something that wasn't there. Then he spoke again.

"Look, we got who we want downstairs. They got records. They don't give a fuck about the future. You ain't like them, and don't let them tell you that you are. All I want from you is to not see you in here again."

I didn't mean to say the words, but they were the only ones in my head, playing over and over again like a disc on repeat. "She's gone."

His eyes softened as the words reached his ears. "Not forever," he replied. "You just made some choices she couldn't agree with. It happens. But it doesn't mean she won't be there for you if you get your life together."

"What is this, an after-school special?" I blurted. I didn't want to feel sorry. I didn't want some fucking cop trying to comfort me. "Since when do cops start givin' a fuck about the people they lock up?"

"Watch your mouth," he said calmly. "I can put you back downstairs. And I can tell by that scared look on your face that that's the last place you wanna be."

He was right. But I wouldn't tell him that. I didn't want to tell him anything at all. I appreciated what he was trying to do, though. It gave me that warm hope I'd missed since Mr. Seasons had been killed. Him talking to me proved that they didn't all look at us like animals, like they were better just because they were on the other side of things. I gave him a nod, hoping he'd know that was all that I could give.

"I'ma let you go," he said. "But your boys down there are another story. We let them go too many times already. And make no mistake—the next time I see you, you'll be on your way to the Tank."

"I don't wanna go there," I said honestly, as I momentarily unlearned all the things that had brought me before Redhead in the first place. He said something else, but I wasn't listening. I didn't want to think about anything anymore, yet I had a brain full of questions.

Where was I going to live? When was the last time I'd been to school? Would Ma ever talk to me again? Would I live to talk to her again if Ray and Troy thought that I'd ratted them out in exchange for my freedom?

Could I go back to being the kid who'd valiantly fought Shaka's boys in hopes of being Chandra's hero, the one who exposed Mr. Seasons's killers? Were those even things that *good* people did?

The questions continued outside of the precinct as I made my way onto New York Avenue and started down toward the library. It was almost eight, and I knew that it'd be closing soon. But I just needed somewhere to sit for a minute where I could soothe the heat coursing through me with some icy air-conditioning and bury all my thoughts in the words on pages.

I stopped liking school, but I never fell out of love with reading. Way after I stopped going to school, I'd still go to the library and grab books off the shelves. I liked stories about other places and books that taught you how to do things and books that made me feel thankful for the life I had, that let me know that things could be so much worse, that I was blessed.

I hid in the library bathroom, then the supply closet, and finally under a table as they shut the place down for the night. I fell asleep after midnight, reading *The Outsider* under the red-bulbed EXIT sign.

I woke up just a little before sunrise. I snuck out through the basement and onto 7th Street. Then I wandered around until familiar faces began to pass on their way to the subway.

Lana let me stay at her and Ray's apartment a few floors down from their mother's. The judge gave Ray and Troy six months each, a punch in the arm instead of the uppercut they needed to truly learn the lesson. So it was just Lana and me for a while. She got me a job at the Cinnabon in Wheaton, and it worked out for a stretch. I aced the GED without even studying.

"You always had more sense than my brother," Lana said one night as she squeezed her wide ass into the chair next to the sofa and cracked open a can of Olde E. "I'm glad to see you usin' it."

"Thanks," I said, not knowing any other way to respond. "I'm just tryin' to be a good boy."

Three weeks later hard times hit the food court and I was a good boy without a check. I looked and looked and nothing opened up, and my small-time money quickly melted into a handful of change. Legal living was an expensive enterprise, and the corners had turned into World War III. A couple of kids had even gotten shot up at my old high school in broad daylight. I couldn't go backward, and there seemed to be nothing but darkness up ahead. So I kind of stood where I was, frozen, until fate once again brought me exactly where I was supposed to be.

Ray kept a .380 pistol taped under the couch in his and Lana's crib. It was supposed to be for emergencies, but I got bored one night and took it out while Lana was at work, tucked it in the back of my Guess, and covered it with my shirt. It was the dead of winter, but I decided to go for a walk.

I walked up 7th until it turned into Georgia Avenue and stopped at the China Wonder carryout over by Howard. The place was packed with those damn college kids and their out-of-town accents. I had two dollars to spare, barely enough for a pair of egg rolls. And yet my eyes were fixed on the huge woks behind the counter, both seemingly filled to the brim with beef, shrimp, and vegetables. Somebody was gonna eat well.

The rolls would only ease the growling in my belly for a little while, maybe just long enough for me to get back to Lana's and go to sleep on that lumpy-ass couch.

So I placed my order and handed over my two little singles. My ears wandered their way from conversation to conversation as I waited. A group of light-skinned girls in turtlenecked sweaters and designer coats laughed amongst themselves as they picked over the full plates before them. One of them scowled in my direction, noting that nappy Afros and worn jeans weren't her thing.

"Can you believe Daddy only sent me a four-hundred-dollar check this month?" the scowling girl posed to her friends, who all seemed even more stunned than she was.

Shit, I couldn't believe it either. First, I didn't know my father, and second, four hundred dollars was rent money, not spending change for some little bitch that lived in a dorm while she got ready for her career as a trophy wife. The pistol at my back whispered something in my ear as the cashier handed me my grease-soaked paper bag. That little gun had a pretty good idea.

Twenty minutes passed before the Hillary Banks quartet left the carryout. It's easy to follow a mark on a college campus. Everybody's slippin', so wrapped up in having a good time and being free from Mommy and Daddy that they don't keep their eyes open as wide as they might back home. They don't look behind them on those dark streets because they're so certain that campus security will ride in with their little golf carts and rescue them.

I'd gone out with a broad from Howard a couple of times, a tiny little thing named Virginia who was from West Virginia. But the good times rolled to an end when she found a few rocks in my jacket. Nonetheless, I knew her dorm. And that was exactly the direction in which the Bel Air girls were heading.

Three of the four peeled off just a block down, heading up the hill toward the center of campus, which was a good thing. Two was a terrific number, particularly on the narrow side street that led to their destination. A lost purse would be nothing but an inconvenience for either of these girls. For me it might be a way to stay alive. I picked up my pace and came down on them like an owl on its prey.

I slipped Ponytail's bag off her arm without her even feeling it. But her four-eyed friend saw me, my features perfectly covered by the hood pulled tightly over my eyes. She went to scream, but the sight of a pistol kept the sound from hitting the air. By the time Ponytail spun around, I was already a third of the way across the unlit parking lot, carrying my very first successful score.

I hadn't said a word. No verbal threats. No knife to the throat or gun to the back or anything that would've scarred them for life. They didn't even know I was there until I was gone. I actually felt kinda proud, proud for the first time in a long time.

I slowed to a stop on the other side of Florida Avenue, just beyond the ocean of crackheads that lived in the buildings there. Looking back, I should have never opened the goods out in public. But I ducked into an alley I knew well and practically tore the bag open. There were five twenties and a ten in the wallet, plus ID and a couple of credit cards. No pictures.

Since I wore gloves, I didn't need to wipe away prints from the bag. I just dropped it in the Dumpster and headed toward home, where I shredded the card in Lana's garbage disposal. It felt good to empower myself. I hadn't planned it. It had just been an impulse, a way to channel all my anger without inflicting pain, without filling out another job application in vain. I'd made the money my way.

Sure, Ma wouldn't have liked it. But she wasn't feeding me anymore. I was on my own, and despite my best intentions, this was all that I could do.

SOUL

"What the fuck happened, Ray?" I yelled. I might have put a gun to his head if we hadn't both dumped our pieces a few minutes earlier.

It was supposed to be so simple, rob the weed spot and get the paper inside of it. I'd committed the layout of the entire store to memory. In the front room there were three aisles full of goods and a counter with a single cashier. The second room at the rear was for "storage" and where two dudes sold smoke to anybody who knew the password.

The door between the two rooms was made of rotting pine, which meant it'd be easy to kick open (or even through) if needed. And only one of the men back there was carrying. We had the gloves, the guns, and the nuts to make it go down lovely. And still, Ray had managed to fuck it up.

"I tripped," he said, his eyes falling to the cracked sidewalk beneath us.

"You tripped?" I asked. By then frustration had filled every cranny of my being. It wasn't that two people, the gun-crazy cashier, and the guy in the back with the MAC-10 and the poor aim, were dead. That was how it went sometimes. What made me salty was the fact that we'd almost lost our lives in the process. That was totally unacceptable.

"How many times we case that muthafuckin' place!? And you fuckin' *tripped*?! How the fuck did you trip?"

"I had my plan together, right," he recounted, rising from the concrete step where he'd parked himself. "I was gonna come in, go to the back like I was getting some chips, and break into a Michael Jackson act right in the middle of the store as a distraction. I figured at least one of the cats from the back would come in just to look, and I could pull out the piece and kill two birds with one stone."

I didn't want to accept the truth for what it was. Ray had brought *me* into the game. He'd had the heart to take a bullet and keep on shooting. But all that aside, he'd never been a criminal mastermind. So when I sent him in to create a diversion, a makeshift King of Pop impression was the best he could come up with. I should have known better.

"So I got me a bag of Doritos, right," he continued, as if it really mattered. "And I was about to turn around when I remembered that I didn't have my mask on yet. And if I didn't pull it up, then ole boy at the counter was gonna know who I was. So I dropped the chips and pulled my mask up and went for my piece. But it slipped out my waist, and I dropped it on the ground. And when I went to go after it, my foot got caught on the potato chip rack and I tripped. And then the rack fell on top of me. But I got to my gun and dude went behind the counter and pulled out his heat. Then the dude wit' the gun from the back came out and the shit just got crazy. Everybody was shootin'. And then you came in."

I had to come in like the cavalry and shoot two people in four seconds, bullets screaming by me while my partner tried to shake his leg out from under the metal rack and bags of chips on top of him. I told myself it was okay, that once upon a time he had given me, the amateur, a shot at making real money moving weight on that corner. Our boy E had moved down to Charlotte. I was all he had left. So I'd asked him to join me in the streets once he came home from Lorton.

We slept and worked out of this little two-bedroom on O Street, less than a block from the playground where we'd met back in the sixth grade. But since then the stakes had risen like mercury. The jobs had become more complicated, and this time Ray's clumsiness had been almost too much to bear.

Everything I did had to be organized. Even back as a hustler, my shifts always ran without a hitch. Maybe I was a perfectionist. Or maybe I still had Redhead's words in my ears. Maybe I was doing everything it took to never end up in a cell again.

I thought like a machine would, eliminating any potential problem before it had the chance to thwart us from getting away clean. It wasn't a game for me. It was my life.

"You gotta be more fuckin' careful!" I yelled at Ray. "It's a lotta shit on the line erry time we do this. I mean, it's two dead niggas back there."

I couldn't remember the counterman's face, the one I'd just aerated with a slug through the skull, his blood splattering across the shelves of cold medicine and deodorant right behind him. I'd breezed by his corpse like it was trash in the wind.

"I know," Ray apologized with this embarrassed look on his face. "You know me. You know I'm a thorough muthafucka."

"Yeah, I know," I replied. "'Cuz if not, I'd be down the alley wit' my half wishin' you the best." He nodded without a word. "Now let's go somewhere where we can count this out."

There was almost four grand in the bag, around what we'd expected for a Tuesday night. Maybe we should have hit them on the weekend. But we figured they would've been a little more prepared then. Of course, the Captain, who ran the operation, would be looking for the culprits. And usually it would be easy to find them.

The usual thieves were the bummy-looking dudes around

the way who all of a sudden turned up in brand new clothes. Their girlfriends showed up at parties and clubs with gold chains and diamond tennis bracelets, getting the full treatment at the salon instead of the usual press and curl.

But that wasn't us. Ray and I had bills to pay. We put the rent and utilities a few months ahead and even bought a piece of the barbershop that had just opened up down by the new Green Line station. We made sure we never fit the description, that we never matched up to anybody's profile. And that had kept us alive where others weren't so lucky.

There had been a little something extra in that bag we lifted, a half brick of the Captain's best green. We split it down the middle. But I didn't smoke. And though the end of the summer was a little cooler than normal, I knew exactly where I could get rid of my share.

"You looking for a bob, main man?" I whispered to the purple-lipped nigga in the Hawaiian shirt. Normally I would've been a little more cautious, but if he wasn't a smoker nobody was.

"How much?" he whispered back, though others could clearly hear us. I wasn't worried about being heard. Park cops were more focused on litter and liquor. I motioned for him to follow me outside, and he walked out two steps behind me.

There was a good crowd of people outside the restrooms, the perfect camouflage for another quick sale. Music echoed up from the speakers down the hill as the saxophonist on stage dropped into a sanctified solo. It was in the low eighties outside, but all the tank tops and shorts would've made you think we were in the middle of a heat wave.

"That shit chocolate?" my colorful customer asked.

"Nah," I said. "Better than that. This dat 'dro shit."

His narrow eyes widened in excitement. "For real?"

"Yup." I gave him the look he needed, the one that told him that I was doing him a favor by even offering him the chance to indulge. Then I let silence hang between us for just the right number of seconds, just enough for him to come to realize that he might be missing out on the puff of a lifetime.

I gave him a good once-over. His cut was up to code and his Tim loafers were brand new. The herringbone around his neck was thick enough to be a collar.

"So how much you want?" I asked again. He tapped his pockets with nervous fingers, still debating, a kid trying to figure out if what I had was worth his whole allowance.

"Fuck it," he said with a smile. "Gimme a half."

"Two hundred," I said. If he bit the bait I'd go home with an extra seven yards in my pocket and no more product to speak of. Friday nights at Dupont Park were a gold mine for this kind of thing.

It didn't take Slim in front of me long to make his decision. He nodded. We made the handoff, and I was ready to go home.

"You always think somebody tryin' to holler!" a dude's voice yelled from a few yards away. I cut my eyes in that direction and found a Larry Johnson lookalike standing in front of a broad who deserved better. Larry's arms were flung wide in a challenge to her. But she didn't seem to be the least bit fazed.

"I seen you with the woman! I seen you trying to talk to her two minutes ago over by the bathroom. It's like this every time we go out. And I'm sick of the shit!"

I needed popcorn. Shit, this was better than the band down the way. But it wasn't his squirming that kept me there. It was her, the way her pretty browns glimmered beneath the streetlights overhead. Her peanut butter thighs descended into calves that stretched on forever. But it was that cocky grin she wore that made me stiffen like cement.

What was she doing with a bama like "Larry Johnson," a man whose game was as loose as the jeans hanging off his ass?

"So what you gonna do?" he dared her. "You know a good thing when you see it. You just gotta learn how to share it."

Her open hand flew at him faster than sound, twisting his chubby face like it was a fist. It seemed like the whole city heard the pop it made. Everything seemed to stop, even the band down the way.

"*That's* what I'm gonna do," she said, rotating her hand to stretch the muscles in her wrist. Her other hand locked onto her hip as she looked up at the incredible shrinking man before her. All eyes were on him.

I hoped that he wouldn't return fire, even though there was nothing I could've done to stop him if he did. It wasn't my business, and I'd learned the hard way to stay out of other people's affairs. But if he left her, that would be another story entirely.

Larry's head drooped as he started past her, dragging himself past the line of cars parked on the shoulder and eventually out of sight. Then came the echoed slamming of a car door and the starting of an engine. He had left her. And she was still standing there.

I could tell that she hadn't expected him to full-out jet. Neither had I. The surrounding crowd swarmed toward her like bees, drowning her with the honey of unneeded "Forget hims" and "Honey, are you alrights." I had to wait until their buzzing had faded, until most had started back toward the stage down the way or their cars to go home. A few dudes stood around on the edges, probably waiting to make some kind of play. But I didn't give them the chance.

She saw my approach long before I touched down and met me halfway.

"They've said it all," she sighed. "I don't think there's much you can add to it."

"You got a ride home?" I asked.

I knew I had her when the corners of her lips curled.

"Well, I guess there is," she replied. Three minutes later we were leaving the park in my Regal.

"Andre doesn't fit you," she said after our unexpected detour to a little bistro called the Market Inn down by the wharf. Glasses of white wine had been ordered, and I sucked my first down quickly, not yet knowing that you weren't supposed to guzzle it like the usual brew.

"Most people call me Snow," I said.

"Snow?" she asked, revealing a light set of dimples just beyond her smile lines.

"Because of this," I said, pointing to my birthmark. "When I was in school, this girl said it looked like a snowflake." She studied the mark for a moment and then nodded in agreement.

"Yeah," she said. "It does."

"So who was he?" I asked.

"Nobody. They're all nobodies. You know, like cutouts of men but not the real thing."

"What do you think a *real* man is?" I asked. Surprisingly, she had an answer ready.

"Someone who cares enough to make sacrifices for somebody other than himself. Somebody who's really willing to love and not just fuck."

"You musta thought about it a lot," I said. "I mean, I wasn't expectin' a answer that involved."

"I'm not what you're used to," she said.

Her name was Adele, and she was from the furthest corner of Northwest, in Takoma Park up off of Blair Road, where they had the nicest houses I'd ever seen. She worked as an accountant for a firm off of H Street and was studying for the CPA exam.

"I think I'm still trying to find myself," she added, running her hand across the short and oiled 'fro that covered her lovely skull.

"What do you do?" she asked. I had to think of a way to phrase it properly.

"I move merchandise," I said.

"What kind?" she asked.

"Whatever kind I come across."

She gave me a wink of recognition. "Oh, one of *those* kinds of guys," she said. "High-risk, high-yield investments?"

"Medium-yield," I replied with a smile. "I ain't been doin' it for that long."

"You'll make your way up the ladder," she said with that cocky grin. "You seem ambitious enough."

And she left it at that. I didn't understand why until months later, when she told me her old man had "moved merchandise" too, and in ways far beyond anything I'd even thought about. The only problem was that he brought the real bacon home to his other family over on the Gold Coast, while she grew up with her mama living in a one-bedroom over a liquor store on MLK in Southeast, not far from where I'd lived back in the Landy days.

I drove her to the steps next to the Rock Creek Parkway, down the street from the Lincoln Memorial, and we talked there for a long time about what it was like to live in the city, and the places we wanted to go and the things we wanted to own. I smiled and laughed more than I had in years. From there we went to Adams Morgan and had drinks at Bukom. The crowd was fixated on the Lakers/Bullets game, but we barely noticed anything but each other.

And then I took her home, or to at least what I thought was her home, an apartment building on Harvard and 15th.

"I'll probably go home tomorrow," she said. "I'll stay at my girl's house tonight."

"I can take you to *your* house, you know?"

"Yes, you could," she said with a sexy grin. "But then you'd know where I live. You have my number, though. That's a start."

I glanced over at the business card she left on the dash, which had slid all the way down against the windshield, just to make sure it was still there.

"Yeah, I got it." I smiled.

"I expect to hear from you within forty-eight hours."

"And I expect you to pick up when I call," I said. I watched her narrow hips switch back and forth and she moved to the apartment entrance and disappeared inside. Her ass was small but as round as an apple. I pulled off toward Florida Avenue, the quickest way to get me home.

I hadn't given much real thought to women in a long time. Like Ray had said, most had convinced me that their only purpose was to keep my dick in shape. But Ms. Adele had a glow that I wanted to stand inside of forever, a warmth that I wanted to possess me late into the night and into the next morning, every morning.

I was pretty sure that she'd play me like a rebound, though, take me for a thug fantasy and run for the border once the dick ran dry. That had happened too many times before. But even if it did again, just the traces of her that remained would be worth more than a lifetime with someone else.

FIRE

The pain came when it wanted to. But the doctors couldn't tell me why. I knew the original cause had been that slug that pierced my shoulder months earlier. But I'd been shot before. And from what I knew, the wounds weren't supposed to ache months after.

Adele made me go to the doctor. Then he made me go to two different specialists. But all of their tests came back negative, the X-rays as normal as *Monday Night Football*. But one of those quacks, the only Black one, said that my problem could be *psychosomatic*, that the pain was all in my head.

I looked "psychosomatic" up in a medical book on one of my Thursday trips to the library. I suppose the doc could have been right. It could have just been in my mind. But I knew that wasn't the case. Shit, I wasn't crazy. I'd hurt enough in my life. The last thing I wanted was to imagine being hurt some more.

But even with the ice packs and heat pads, the electric massagers and the way Adele would bite on the muscle, erecting other parts of me at the same time, that nagging pain still reared its head every once in a while. And I felt it start to burn just as my boy Ray pulled the top off a Heiny and brought it out to the back porch.

"I don't know how you keep doin' it," he said as he slouched in the flimsy deck chair. I looked beyond my old partner to stare at the wife on the other side of the screen door, holding Kayi high in the air. She had just started to crawl, and it was a struggle to keep her from wandering to the other side of town if I looked away for too long.

"What you mean?" I asked in reply, downing the last of my own green-bottle brew.

"I mean still bein' out there," he said, removing a faded blue postman's cap to scratch his balding head. "You got a kid now and all. How come you don't worry about not comin' back?"

"I just always make sure that I do. No matter what happens to me, I'm gonna make it back home. That's the one promise I always gotta keep." He looked at me like I'd told him a lie without meaning to.

Ray might have known me better than anybody, even my best friend, Thai. He knew because there had been a time when we were two peas in a pod, back when our game seemed new, back when we did what we did half the time just for fun. We didn't owe anybody shit. So we walked around figuring we'd never have anything to lose.

Then Ray had Brianna when he was twenty-three. And that (along with him just being no fuckin' good at it anymore) was his cue to lay the life to rest.

"It ain't always up to you," Ray said sternly. "Sometimes your number just be up."

"It ain't my time yet," I said, painting my face with a grin as I flashed back to the night that girl had clipped me in the shoulder while those apartment curtains burned to a crisp behind us. I'd drilled through her heart with a single shot, leaving her newly orphaned infant to find her way in the world alone. All for five grand, five thousand measly Georges.

That night was bothering me in a way nothing ever had

before. Once upon a time I had been a nigga that might have laughed at the fear on a mark's face as he fell to the floor full of holes. But now the Mel Gibson was running out of me. And I wasn't sure how I felt about it.

Yeah, it was a two-job household. Adele was an accountant. She cleaned up books and ledgers for the kind of people who couldn't go to H&R Block. And I did what I did. Between the two of us we'd made a nice little life for the three of us, a life that was free of the things I'd known at home, the smell of urine in the hallways, the broken glass all over the playground, the graffiti lists of names that only got longer as the years went on. We were already beyond the echoes of shots fired between friends and foes. And the plan was to take us even further out of range. Maybe I'd move them to PG or Gaithersburg. Shit, Great Falls if it all came together right. The whole thing was for my family to be safe, for none of us to ever have to worry about the other not being there anymore.

"That's what they all said," Ray grunted as he looked me dead in the face. Then he sighed and looked at his watch. "But I'm 'bout to head out. This late shift is a bitch. But at least I know erry night is gonna be the same, though."

His words hit like a hollow tip, slicing to shreds my carefully built illusion, the living meditation that had pushed all my stress and worries into some cul-de-sac at the back of my brain. He knew me too well. And he could tell I was losing it.

I'm sure Ray thought that was a good thing. I hugged him like a brother before I watched his Pathfinder pull off toward the main post office on Brentwood. Then I checked my own watch. I had to get to work too.

"You know what thermite is?" Kamau asked me in the back of the Jiffy Laundromat on 7th. There was a brick of white on the table big enough to OD half the neighborhood.

"Nah," I said, still curious as to what he'd asked me there for. He reached into the box under the table and came up with something that looked like an oversized saltshaker with some kind of a metal rig at the top.

"Shit is like some kinda explosive," he said, rubbing his freshly shaved cheek. "Supposed to be so hot it'll burn through anything. It's like some Navy Seals shit. Can't get it on the street if you tried. But you know my little cousin learned how to make it off the Internet?"

The mischief in his smile made me nervous.

Kamau had been oil on water in the past few months, floating to the top of things after I'd offed his only two superiors at the same card game where I'd gotten clipped in the shoulder. His boy Mike Mike, the lookout that night, hadn't been so lucky. He still wasn't walking right after the lead-pipe discipline he'd been given for telling me where the game was in the first place. Maybe that should have worried me, but it didn't.

The neighborhood was changing. The white folks from downtown were slithering in like thieves in the night. The fiends and addicts were all getting pushed into Kamau's territory, putting him on the yellow brick road to easy street.

So he'd asked me to come see him. He said that he wanted the two of us to figure out a way to keep money in both our pockets. I wasn't big on working for anybody long term. But I knew that Kamau could keep the green in my safe thicker than the metal it was made of.

"That some of it right there?" I asked, curious about the thermite.

"Yup. And I'm keeping it to myself. People get outta line, I'm blowing up they buildins."

He let out a deep laugh, his head jerking back so hard that the horn-rimmed glasses on his face went crooked.

"You gotta do what you gotta do," I said.

"And I know that's right," he coughed, his eyes starting to tear from laughing so hard.

"So what you need?" I asked. It was getting late, and I couldn't wait to get back to the house, back to the warmth of my two ladies and the Mavericks game that started at nine.

"What only you can give me," he smiled. "I need you to watch my boy's back,"

"Which boy?"

"Kenny. You know Kenny, right?"

"You mean Kofi's little brother? He's with you now?"

"Hell, yeah." Kamau beamed proudly. "He know who the winners is. But anyway, I got him making a deal for me." He took a moment to slide a stick of gum between his fuchsia-colored lips.

"What kinda deal?" I asked.

"What difference it make? You ain't dealin'. You just shootin' if some shit jump off."

He had a point, and I nodded to let him know it.

"Thing is, it's on a boat. It's on the *Spirit*."

"That one that leaves from down by the waterfront?"

Kamau nodded. "Yeah, it's a cabaret on there tonight."

"How much?"

"Forty," he grunted, as if it hurt him to say the word. It was a better number than the one on my tongue's tip. Shit, that was half of what Adele made in a year.

"When?" I asked, still wearing my poker face.

"Tonight at eleven. Meet him down at L'Enfant Plaza in front of HUD. You know what he look like, right?"

"I want half up front," I said, locking my eyes with his.

"I'm one step ahead of you." He reached underneath the desk to produce a thick manila envelope sealed closed, which he handed to me. "I'ma always take care of business."

We shook hands, the seal of a deal, and I left out the back and through the laundromat entrance. The place was packed for a Tuesday night, with twenty or thirty people standing and sitting, their hands gripping quarters and bottles of detergent in hopes of getting their drawers clean. I nodded to a few of them, remembering the faces more than the names. In twenty-five years, I'd learned a lot about my neighbors without them learning half as much about me.

"One of us has to go to the supermarket," Adele said, zipping up a fresh pair of skintight jeans, her little ass forming a near-perfect bubble in the fabric.

The jeans were the third step in her unwinding-from-work process. The first was always a glass of merlot, followed by hanging up her suit and ten minutes of meditation. Then came the jeans. I personally never understood how the girl could relax in pants that tight. But then again I was only the man she'd married.

I had Kayi down in the living room, tossing her in the air like a sack of flour. Her laugh made the ice inside me melt.

"What you need?" I asked her, remembering the almost two hundred dollars I'd spent at the supermarket just a few days before.

"Tampons," she said plainly, her back to me as she pulled a Clark Atlanta T-shirt over her tiny-nippled breasts. "You always forget."

"Is this like *pressing*?" I asked, glancing at the clock in the kitchen. It was already six-thirty, which meant I barely had enough time to lift. "You know I'm workin' tonight."

. The look she gave me said that I was being insensitive.

But I didn't want to tell her that I was too embarrassed to admit that I still felt funny when I brought Tampax up to the checkout.

"Well, my *friend's* comin' soon," she said. "So if you can't go now, at least bring them in later on tonight."

"I promise," I said, unhappy with the fact that I'd probably have to make a run for feminine products at four in the morning, when there'd only be a single checkout open and twenty people in front of me.

"Come here," she said, tapping the space on the mattress next to her. I moved to the designated spot.

"Wassup?" I asked. She slid a hand onto a hip, staring me down for a moment with narrowing eyes.

"Is this one worth it?" she asked, running her gentle hand across my unshaven cheek.

Adele knew who I was. She had always known. Love was the most difficult score of all, though, particularly holding onto the merchandise.

"Definitely," I said in response to her question. She gave me a suspicious look as she took Kayi up to the bedroom. *Buffy* came on soon, and she never missed an episode. I headed for the basement.

I counted out the twenty grand and put it in the safe behind the dryer. That made seventy for the quarter, which wasn't too bad. Then I did forty-five on the bike, a few sets on the bench, some crunches, curls, and leg lifts. By the time I was done, it was eight. After a shower, I had to do fifty in the city just to make it to the waterfront in time. I wanted to check it all out before anyone else got there.

The only problem with working alone is not having anybody to watch your back. I usually didn't need it. But it had always been good to know that Ray was out there on the other end of a radio or sitting behind the wheel with the motor running or pointing his .45 wherever I needed it to be.

So when he left, I just grew eyes in the back of my head. I had to feel someone coming up behind me. I had to hear the slight change in a voice that came just before it told me a lie. I became self-contained, with enough aim and ambition to keep it that way.

There were two big boats in the moonlit harbor: The *Spirit of Washington* and another, smaller, yacht. The little one was dark and dead. But the *Spirit* was jumping, colored lights flashing to the beats that boomed out of every one of its openings.

A line of thirty-somethings dressed to impress had formed right next to the loading ramp. There were two bouncers at the entrance, and another two on the *Spirit*'s deck leading people into the main party area. I knew that some of them would be carrying. But Kamau had told me I wouldn't be searched. So that was less of an issue.

There was only one way on and off the boat without getting wet. Ten lifeboats were on the top deck in case of emergency. Forty grand a night was too much to pay somebody, even for a location that well secured. Then again, I wasn't sure about who Kenny was dealing with or what might be bought or sold. Too many blanks in an equation made me nervous. But my nerves knew their place, particularly when it came to the money.

I got back in the Regal and cruised down the waterfront to L'Enfant Plaza station. Kenny was pacing by the mall exit like a little girl waiting on her prom date, his short, pudgy frame bulging out of a leather trench and matching boots. The bottom of the coat was too big for him, so that it dragged on the ground as he walked. Kenny's face looked like he'd just been told he was going to the gas chamber.

"You ready?" I asked as I shifted into first.

"Yeah," he replied nervously. "What you know?"

"That I'm supposed to make sure nobody fucks with you."

"Yeah, that's about right," he said with a forced grin. "Just follow me, and I'll do the talkin'."

"So where to now?" I asked.

"To the boat," he said. "To the boat." It wasn't good when a person repeated himself.

I turned up the 911 tape and let the music thump through my speakers. I needed to get that feeling again, the one that had gotten me through all of my bloody nights and guiltless mornings. But it was getting harder. I hoped that the music would help. But bass and treble couldn't wash it all away the way it used to.

"Stay behind me," Kenny said as I power-locked the doors. I scanned the immediate area and locked onto the group of men at the edge of the parking lot. They were just beyond the line of partygoers packing its way onto the big boat. "That's them over there," he smirked.

Kenny was one of Kamau's newest boys. So this was the first thing Kamau was letting him handle on his own. I barely knew him myself, only that he was the little brother of a dude who got a football scholarship to Central only to get shot trying to break up a fight before he could cash it in.

Kenny was always on the scene, always peering over somebody else's shoulder trying to make it into somebody else's snapshot. He definitely wasn't the trigger-pulling type. Nor had he ever been somebody that gave orders. He just floated through it all, picking up enough cash to keep on living. Bottom line was that I didn't trust him, even if I was on the payroll.

There were five of them bunched together, all bearded, and not a single one under six feet. Sure, I could've taken them head-on: broken some knees, crushed a testicle, whatever. Or I could've just started blasting, whatever it took to keep Kenny alive. But that was only if there was a problem, and thus far there wasn't even a trace of one.

But all that changed when I heard the slamming of car doors behind me. The approaching footsteps were somehow a dead giveaway that I'd walked into a trap. Kenny spun around and pulled at the pistol in his waistband, but he couldn't get it free. My Sigs were already gripped.

#1 put a hole in the center of his skull, and he fell face forward. The bearded men behind him froze for a moment. Then they raised their weapons. I hit two of them in the chest and rolled to my left, just fast enough to avoid the bullets coming from behind me, which managed to shred the beards who were about to be in my way. Amateurs.

I dropped and rolled again, barely avoiding the next wave of lead. As I got back to my feet, I only knew that I had to run. My arms were too short to box with that many guns, even with Kevlar and extra clips. I gripped my guns like they were trying to get away from me.

The enemy came up behind me fast as I slipped my pistols back into the pockets of my leather so the bouncers wouldn't see them. But the goons grabbed for me anyway as I started toward the entrance ramp. They went to the right, and I cut left, using one of their shoulders to vault over the railing. Somebody was going through an awful lot of trouble to wipe me off the earth's surface.

A bullet shattered the floodlight a few feet in front of me. I ducked into the main cabin, where the dance floor was, the screams of panicking partygoers ringing through the air all around me.

The dance floor was clearing as people ran every which way. The DJ hit the deck when he saw me coming with the others behind me. But I didn't give a damn about him. I was eyeing the open window on the other side of the room. Several more slugs tomahawked past me as I cut from side to side, refusing to make it easy for them to get off a clean shot.

The window didn't lead to the outer deck of the ship. If I climbed through it blindly, I'd probably have landed in the disgusting water below. It was a good thing that I spotted the smaller yacht at the next dock, the upper deck of which was only about five or six feet over. I pushed my quads until they burned.

I came close to human flight as I sailed across the gap, bending my knees to brace for impact on the smaller ship. The drop nearly sprained both my ankles, but I kept my attention on the window I'd just come through. Armed silhouettes appeared there seconds later, and #2 gave each several wounds through their torsos. At least one thing had gone as planned.

But watching them fall almost cost me wounds of my own. TEC-9 fire hit the deck by my feet, and I scrambled backward. I put #2 in my pocket and tried the boat door. It was locked. A round meant for my head then blew that lock into a million pieces.

The slugs swarmed at me like roaches, coming in from everywhere. The cabin door slid open, and I scrambled into the shadowy vessel. How many of them were out there?

I didn't have time to look for a light switch as even more bullets punched through the glass behind me. Two figures came toward the doorway, and I pumped a few in their direction. Then I made a break for the stairs to the lower deck with nothing but a few scattered rays of moonlight to guide me. I got down there and reloaded, stuffing the empty clips into my coat. Never leave evidence if you don't have to.

There were more footsteps on the deck above. I'd never been up against this many soldiers. Fear wiggled its way

into my thought process. I backed up to the end of the hallway. They were going to have to come and get me. Two
pairs of feet started down the steps, and I sent slugs their
way. A bullet snapped the bone of an ankle before it was
pulled out of view. And then there was silence, deafening silence.

A single sound broke the pause. Something was rolling
down the stairs, picking up speed as it moved toward me.
My hand found the hall light switch at just the right moment, and I flipped it on.

The corridor came alive, and I saw the tiny cylinder as it
thumped slowly down the staircase. It looked like a saltshaker
with some kind of a metal rig on top. The wick was burning
down to nothing. I backed up as far as I could. I'd never
said a prayer before, at least not on the job. But I asked God
for some kind of deliverance as I covered my ears. This might
have been the night I would break my nightly promise.

The explosion made me blind and deaf for a moment or
two. Then I saw the huge crater in the deck floor. The water
was up to my ankles in less than a second, to my knees two
seconds after that. I sloshed toward the stairway and
sprinted to the upper deck, but a rain of bullets sent me
back down below. They'd been playing the quiet game just
to make certain that I couldn't get out when the time came.

The good thing was that they couldn't stand there forever, at least not if they wanted to live. The bad thing about
that was that they weren't in the bottom of a sinking ship. I
trudged through the rising filth and splintered wood and
fiberglass coming through the gash in the ship's hull.

If there was one thing I'd learned from Ray, it was that
you had to be ready for anything. That was why I took
swimming classes at Capitol East one summer. I dropped #1
and #2 on the deck and peeled off my leather. I pulled off

my boots and hooked my car keys to my belt loop. Then I went straight into the icy water, figuring I had a better chance against hypothermia than the hollow-tipped therapy still waiting for me upstairs.

I once read somewhere that the will to survive is stronger than anything else, and as I swam out through the breech in the boat's belly, I kept picturing Adele's face, thinking of her and me in our bed and the warmth she always brought to blood that used to run cold in my veins. I thought of my mother truly loving me again. And I thought of Kayi and the way I swore to be there for her for the rest of my hopefully long life. Thinking those thoughts made the rest of it easy. I punched through the scum's surface just as I started to feel dizzy from running out of air.

The boat was halfway under when my eyes came into focus. A sea of red and blue lights had inundated the dock's parking lot. Cops had already begun to question the line of partygoers and examine the bodies I'd left for them. Three ambulances were parked in strategic relation to the bodies. But there were no more bearded men in sight, at least none that were moving.

My Regal was parked on the edge of it all, just far enough away from the commotion for me to reach it without being spotted. Being that wet in the cold had me feeling sick almost instantly as I hid behind a parked Maxima wagon very similar to one I'd owned when I was younger. It wasn't long before I started to shiver violently, almost like something you'd see in a cartoon. The often-overwhelming heater in my Regal was the only thing that kept me alive as I started back home.

My shoulder was on fire as I passed the Capitol, all the traffic lights a continuous stream of green. The pain was so sharp I had to struggle not to swerve. I tried not to think about what had just happened. I was soaking wet. My head hurt. I should've been dead. I should have been dead long before any of this.

But what I had to focus on were the facts. First, that the other half of my twenty grand was never going into the safe. Second, that someone may have fed a description of me to the cops. And third, that Kamau had thirty-four bullets coming to him via Snowflake Express.

I needed my lady. I needed to go home and make love to her. I had to whisper how much she meant to me as I felt her tighten around my erection, always doing whatever it took in that space to make me feel perfect.

The demons that had fueled me for so long had grown tired, weak. The hunger wasn't enough to move the Snowmobile. I had enough money to walk away from it all, right then and there. We could leave in the morning, rent out the house and go somewhere else, to Virginia or Pennsylvania, maybe even stay with my boy down in Charlotte.

I could start the auto detail business I'd always thought about, or at least put together a team of young bucks to start doing my work for me. There were so many options. And on the drive up Georgia Avenue, I thought about all of them for the first time since I ran a bag of rocks to a hustlers' spot for two hundred dollars. I finally saw that bigger picture my best friend, Thai, had always talked about. What he and Enrique and all my old girls used to say was beginning to make sense. Even Adele couldn't argue with wanting me to cut down on all the risks.

Then I thought about Kamau and what he was doing, more than likely running his mouth off to his boys about giving me a Navy funeral at the expense of someone else's boat. I thought about how close he came to taking me away from my wife and little girl forever. I couldn't be stupid. Any dreams of going straight were on hold until my score was settled. The clock on the dash said twelve-twenty. I still had time.

The living room was dead and empty as I walked through it, shivering uncontrollably. I stumbled up the stairs as quietly as I could, praying that I didn't wake my little girl. In the bathroom I turned the water up so high it was almost scalding and then stripped down as fast as I could, though wet fabric takes forever to get out of.

The heat curled through me as I submerged myself, its texture warming everything down to the marrow in my bones. The chills of sickness burned away. I closed my eyes, wishing that I didn't have to leave, that I didn't have to go back out into the night. Then the bathroom door clicked open. It was Adele.

My wife stood there in one of my white sleeveless T-shirts and her Tweety pajama bottoms. She looked more worried than she did when Kayi had the measles.

"Oh my God!" she shouted as she rushed over to the tub. "What happened to you?" At first I didn't get it. She'd seen my skin pierced with gaping bullet wounds and blade slashes. She had wrapped sprains and watched doctors set broken bones. "What did they do to you?"

"Somebody sunk a boat with me in it," I said. She was supposed to laugh, but the worry was dripping from her face. She eased her slender arm into the water and took my hand in hers. The water dampened the front of her T-shirt, giving me a clear view of my favorite titties in the world.

"What the hell are you doing in the tub?"

"Tryin' to beat pneumonia," I said.

"That's not what I mean and you know it," she fired back. Her hand unclasped with mine and began to caress my right thigh.

"Look, this is what I do," I said, trying to be nonchalant. I wanted to act like all those thoughts of change hadn't raced through my mind, like it was just another night, just a little thing that hadn't worked out. "You knew that from jump. You said you were cool with it."

"Yeah, I was," she said. "In the beginning. But it's not like it was before. Somebody tried to kill you tonight."

"People try to kill me every night," I yelled back, fighting off another fit of shivering. I plunged deeper into the liquid and warmed it away. "You just don't see the shit!"

"Don't raise your voice," she said calmly.

"I thought you were used to this," I pleaded. "You said you didn't mind this kinda life." The burn in my shoulder intensified.

"Well, I do now," she huffed.

Adele's words made me think about our vows and everything I'd promised in taking them. I was arguing a point that I knew was wrong. And all she wanted was for me, for us, to be safe.

"You're right," I said, touching her cheek with a warm and wet hand. "This shit is gettin' outta hand. But let me take care of it. I promise. I'm done when this is over."

It wasn't a lie. It was more of a hope for something that didn't stand a chance of happening. Or at least I thought it didn't. She undressed and climbed into the tub, her muscular thighs straddling me.

"Did you get the tampons?"

They had barely crossed my mind. "Nah, but I'll go out as soon as I get dressed."

She smiled.

"I knew you were gonna forget." Then she pecked me on the forehead and wrapped her arms around me.

I didn't want to leave. I didn't ever want to go back out again. But I had scores to settle. I was going to let Kamau relax for the night. Let him think that his trap had snapped my neck in two.

SNOW

We dried off and got wet again making slippery on the Posturepedic across the hall from where our daughter slept. I tried to make Adele feel all the things that I could never express in words before her *friend* came and she deprived me for the week. Then I got dressed and returned to the streets of Northwest DC for cigarettes, her tampons, and the two new Sigs I needed to bring the night's business to a close.

EARTH

There was a dull pain in my index finger as I lined up the target in the crosshairs. Arthritis. The things mothers give to their babies.

He was on the roof of the four-story across the street, the house Kamau used to get his product to his many different franchises. The air was icy, the perfect climate for revenge. He didn't see me, a mistake he wouldn't get the chance to make up for.

I wasn't myself as I lay there on my belly, gravel rubbing against my torso, taking aim. My brain fluttered with even more things that hadn't mattered before. How long had this dude lived? Did he have a family? Did he even know what Kamau had done to me? Nevertheless, I had a job to do, and *my* life wasn't the only one depending on it being done right.

Armed lookouts stood on each floor of the house, their silhouettes visible through the open windows. Another four were in the two parked jeeps out front. The man on the roof had to go first. I couldn't afford any advance warnings.

The rain came down in a nasty mist from the dark gray sky above. I'd covered myself with an army-style poncho to keep the water off of my scope. I couldn't see his face, just the outline of his burly frame one hundred yards out. He stood as still as a statue, cradling his AK-47 like it was a sleeping baby. I aimed for the sweet spot just above the bridge of his nose.

The plastic soda bottle shredded like cheese as it muffled the shot. Homemade silencers worked like a charm, even if they only lasted for a single use. I laid the rifle down and stuffed two extra clips into the pockets of my fleece. I'd grabbed a spare pair of Sigs from my stash over by the reservoir.

I scaled down the fire escape to the street and put the rifle back in my Regal's trunk. Kamau had to die. That's all there was to it.

I lit the fuse on the pipe bomb as my feet covered the distance between the Regal and the open basement window. It had burned down halfway by the time I finger-rolled the explosive into the glass opening. Car doors flung open behind me. The four men in the jeeps had apparently figured out what I was up to.

I drew my Sigs. My first slug bludgeoned one at his right temple. I hit another through the breastbone, causing his chest to explode like a melon. I nailed a third in the gut, with a follow-up that grazed his left ear. The last one made a run for it, into the very basement where I'd just tossed the homemade explosive. I raced back across the street to get out of blast range and counted down the final seconds.

"Ka-*Boom!!!*" The concrete rattled as if Godzilla were walking on it. Flames punched through every pane of glass on the basement level. I had watched Kamau's men stack ether tanks against the front basement wall an hour earlier. That just wasn't a good idea.

I could hear their screams inside the burning building, the screams of lives racing toward the end of their line. That's what they got for playing on the wrong team.

Four more men armed with pistols and sawed-offs spilled out of a side entrance. I shoved the pistol in my left hand into my fleece. Then I pulled the pin on a concussion grenade and sent it to them like a Doug Williams pass. It blew them everywhere. Loose parts, including several fingers, rained down on the concrete right in front of me. I could still hear the fading screams of men broiling down in the basement. And I wasn't finished yet.

Then I heard a small child crying off in the distance. At first I thought it was just my mind playing tricks on me. But then came the chattering of other voices, all right behind me. I spun around to see at least ten witnesses: some homeless, others fiends, others passersby who had ducked for cover when the butchering began.

It was just then that I remembered I wasn't back in Shaw, where people knew how to keep their mouths shut. So it was a good thing that the cloak had kept my face from public view. I slipped all the weapons back into my fleece just as the echo of sirens hit the streets. With that I returned to the shadows of the abandoned buildings.

I dumped the cloak in the trunk as a cool drizzle wandered down my scalp and onto my face. It made me feel better than I had in hours. But I still didn't feel good.

I turned the key in the ignition, and my Regal crept down the alley with its headlights off. It was five-thirty in the morning and I had too much on my mind, which made it the perfect time for some breakfast.

"What you do?" Spivy asked me, his back to my front on the other side of the counter. "You must work nights, 'cuz ain't nobody get up this early that don't." He poured the batter onto the sizzling griddle and then added two sausage patties.

"Sometimes I can't sleep," I said. "I go for a run or drive around. Sometimes I come here."

"That still don't answer my question," he replied, turning around so his eyes could meet mine. His mustache and beard had become more salt than pepper in recent years, signs that we were both getting older.

"I'm a courier for this delivery company," I said. The smell of sausages and flapjacks made my muscles relax. The words began to flow more easily. "People send me to get stuff for them in the places they don't wanna go."

"Is that right?" Spivy asked, giving me a look that said he knew the real deal. "Sounds like it could be some money in that."

"Hell yeah," I said. He put a steaming cup of raspberry tea in front of me.

"You still don't drink coffee, huh?" he asked.

"You ask me that every time I'm in here," I replied. "Coffee fucks with my stomach."

"So does bein' up this early," Spivy said with a smile. Then he wiped his shaved dome with the edge of the gray hand towel that never fully left his shoulder.

"Then why you do it?" I asked curiously.

"Well," he said, pausing to take a sip from a mug with the letters "H.N.I.C." on it. He sat his cup down and flipped my breakfast over. "This is the best way for me to handle my business," he said plainly. "I got to take care of things before the big rush around seven."

It was a good story, but that wasn't it. Spivy used to run the numbers, and even a little weed, years before I had been born. And he'd put more than a few people in coffins. But then the riots came, and they turned U Street into ten blocks of barbecue after Martin Luther King got killed. That glimpse of Hell on Earth had been enough to make Spivy go straight.

He took all the money he had put away and bought a building at Florida and Trinidad. Eventually he opened up Spivy's Grill on the bottom floor and lived up top. Everybody knew that story, because he told it to anyone who'd listen on those summer Sunday nights when he'd park his drop-top DeVille in front of the Shaw playground and play Archie Bell like it was still in style.

Spivy had been in knife fights and beatdowns. He'd hit a cop over the head with a garbage can and never got busted for it. People talked about him like he was something out of a comic book.

Sarah Vaughan wound through the air as he wiped down the counter that stretched the length of the place. The top shined in the glow of the exposed bulbs overhead.

I'd told Adele that I was walking away from the life. But I wasn't sure of what I was walking toward. I didn't want to cook people's breakfast like Spivy. Yet there was only so much that I knew how to do after running the streets for so long. I'd read plenty. But without a diploma there was little I could do to prove it.

I didn't want to work for anybody else anyway. What I really wanted was my own set of businesses: a car wash and a barbershop like the one me and Ray had a piece of back in the day. Those kinds of operations stayed packed and, if you set them up right, had the kind of style and flavor that everybody wanted a piece of.

I even thought about putting them together in one building. That way I could give customers two services in the same location. That would've been something my mother could've been proud of, something that would bring her to see me more often than Christmas and Thanksgiving (when she allowed me to come through because she'd "go to Hell" if she didn't see her grandchild).

It shouldn't have taken me that long to do the right thing. It should've all changed the minute Kayi slid through Adele's birth canal. But I had been too selfish then. I'd spent so much time looking out for me that I figured I should've been able to still do it my way, especially since the wife hadn't minded.

But the truth was that it had never been safe for any of us. What if trouble had somehow found its way to our home? What if somebody better than me came along, somebody who could take it all away in a flash? Where had my head been? Where was my heart?

With all the money I'd had, I could've already built something that would've made me a millionaire. It couldn't take too much to get a car wash/barbershop started, less than $200,000 even if I bought the property instead of renting it.

But I didn't believe in banks and loans. And they wouldn't believe in giving me their venture capital anyway. So I knew that I had to get the start-up money from somewhere. But first I had to finish things with Kamau.

There were only two booths in Spivy's, and his customers rarely used them. For most his place was just a carryout. They paid for a greasy bag of food and then snatched off into the day or night. I, on the other hand, always stayed and ate. There was something about Spivy. It seemed like we were kindred spirits.

"The night don't ever get outta you," he said, shaking his head as he flipped my jacks for the last time, then dropped them on a platter with the spicy meat and set it all in front of me.

"Want juice?" he asked. I nodded with a mouthful of sausage as I poured syrup on my hotcakes. The burn in my gut quickly subsided. The added tang of the orange juice cleared my head.

It was good to see that Spivy had made it to be an old man. He gave me hope that the streets would let you live if you threw in the towel and didn't try to be the king forever. Then I thought about Adele and how she wanted the towel in faster than I could throw it. Thinking of my other half made me wonder why Spivy had never mentioned a wife.

"Why you ain't married?" I asked. The weight of the pistols made my fleece heavy.

"You just fulla questions today, huh?"

"Must be the full moon," I said with a grin.

"Wasn't no full moon last night," he said, grinning back. Then he turned serious. "Every woman I lay down with know what I is. A woman wants somebody that's gonna be there. I wasn't that man when I shoulda been. Just missed the bus, I guess."

His eyes went sad as I stuffed forkful after forkful between my lips.

"Ain't never too late for love," I said. "Real playas live forever."

"But they all get tired of playin'," he said. "I'll be back."

He disappeared into the storage area behind the counter. I kept eating, munching on his words along with the breakfast. I finished eating just as his head peeked through the back doorway. I needed to leave.

"How much?" I asked.

"Three," he said plainly. "You headin' home?"

"Yeah," I said, leaving a ten under the saltshaker next to my plate. "Gotta see my babies, both of 'em."

He started toward me but stopped short halfway. "Stay out of trouble," he said. "If you can."

I nodded as I turned my back to head out the door. His eyes burned against the back of my neck until I was out of range.

It was after six when I got home. The brightening orange on the horizon marked the beginning of a Thursday. Exhaustion was a two-ton trailer on my back as I made my way up the stairs to Kayi's room. I could barely keep my eyes open once I got there.

I almost had a heart attack when I peered into the crib to see her one-year-old eyes open-wide and looking right up at me. I picked her up and enclosed her in my tired arms. Her little left foot brushed against the weight of the gun in my right pocket. I held her to me, rocking her back and forth until I was on the verge of collapse. That was our quality time. I kissed her on the forehead and put her back down, certain that I'd be unlucky enough to have her start crying the minute I tried to leave. But she didn't, and I joyfully headed across the hall to my own bedroom.

Adele snored heavily on her side of the bed, her narrow frame wrapped in her favorite Snoopy comforter. I climbed onto the mattress and wrapped myself around her, the scent of Flowerbomb all over the sheets.

"I love you, baby," I whispered.

"I know," she murmured. That was the last thing I remembered.

I didn't hear Adele's alarm go off, and I didn't hear the door close as she took Kayi to her mother's on the way to work. By the time I got up, the midday sun was beaming onto me through the cracked bedroom window. The sting of a sore throat was more than apparent. I couldn't remember another morning when I hadn't gotten up to see them off.

I got out of bed and stretched on the rug in the living room. Then I went into the kitchen to make tea and discovered a one-sentence note taped to the refrigerator door. It read:

We're having dinner at the Market Inn at 8 PM.
—Adele

It wasn't like the wife to actually ask if I was free. As far as she was concerned, everything else came second to her. If she wanted to go to Mars, I'd better have a fueled spaceship ready for whenever she wanted to leave. And eight PM only left me with a few hours to work. I needed to find out where Kamau was. And there was only one person I could get to tell me.

Mike Mike was holed up in his mother's apartment off New Jersey Avenue, right across the street from Dunbar High School. Two men with freshly trimmed beards pretended to be hanging out in front of the three-story building. But I knew who they were and what they were there for. I avoided the confrontation and used the fire escape in back.

The bass from a Brand New Heavies CD rattled the walls of his tiny bedroom. I watched from the window as he bobbed his head back and forth to the music. He didn't hear me when I opened the unlocked window, or the quiet click of Sig #1 as I removed the safety. He didn't get the picture until I hit the off button on the remote control that was balanced on the back of the sofa, just behind his head.

I saw that his right leg was still in a brace as I eased the 9mm barrel just in front of his left ear. He couldn't reach the .380 he had on the table.

"Where is he?" I asked, still standing behind him. But he knew who was speaking.

"Who?" he replied in a poor attempt at playing dumb. I brought the butt of the pistol down against the back of his head, knocking his glasses into his lap. Then I put the gun back to his melon.

"Let's try it again," I said after a sigh.

"Kamau almost killed me because of your ass! That muthafucka broke my leg in two places!"

"Only 'cause you let him, " I said nonchalantly. "I popped

111

Jimmy and Delante in that card game. That made it open season on anybody who wanted to run shit. You coulda been holdin' that pipe insteada gettin' hit wit' it. But I'm tired of fuckin' wit' you, Mike. Tell me where he is."

"You act like you wasn't in the wrong! You set his cousin on fire and popped the other one in the head *two* times."

"What?" I asked confusedly. I stood up and walked around the sofa to look him in his froggish face. He shrank back when he saw me.

"Delante was Kamau's cousin. You ain't know that? Told all of us that twenty G's was a small price for puttin' a hole in yo' ass."

So Kamau's attempted hit had been payback for his cousin. I was actually surprised. And it took a lot to surprise me. His stunt at the waterfront had been the closest anybody had ever come to taking me out. If he tried again, I might not be so lucky.

"He know you was behind that shit last night," Mike added. "You cost that nigga like a half a million."

I was annoyed that the damage hadn't been more. I aimed my piece directly at Mike's leg, the one he didn't have in a brace.

"Where is he?" I asked again. "Unless you want crutches for Christmas." His eyes widened at the very idea of me doing it, which he knew I would. I pulled back the hammer and Mike sang like Anita Baker.

"Adams Morgan. 1949 Columbia Road," he said rapidly. I should've left him with a flesh wound just for the hell of it. But I had what I wanted. I started to exit.

"It's gonna keep goin' on," he said plainly. "You can't stop it." A strange chill ran through me.

"Whatever," I said, playing it off. Then I started toward the window I'd used as an entrance, stopping to pick up

Mike's pistol on the way, just to make sure he didn't try anything.

"Stay outta trouble," I said as my left foot landed on the iron fire escape. "'Cuz you're right. I can't stop 'til I finish it.

"We're going to have two glasses of Sauvignon Blanc," Adele said softly, "and the mussels to start."

We always had the mussels, going back to the first time we'd eaten there. I looked across the table at the woman I'd married. Her blouse and skirt were the same shade of cranberry. The material still hugged her slight curves. My wool sportcoat made the back of my neck itch as our waiter arrived with two glasses of white wine, our mussels, two bowls, and a dish of melted butter.

"To night and day, and the way they complement each other," she said as we raised our glasses. We took a few sips and dug in.

"So," she said with a slight pause. "Is it done?"

I knew what she meant. But I didn't want to talk about it. "Is what done?"

Her eyes narrowed, which meant I'd pissed her off. "I'll take that as a no," she said, tossing aside an empty shell. A soft piano played in the background. "Did I just imagine the conversation we had last night?"

To her, killing Kamau must have seemed like something she could have done on her lunch break.

"Look, you wanna do it for me?" I asked sarcastically.

"Don't make me get loud," she warned. "There's no need for it. All I want is for Kayi to see you on her second birthday."

"I hear you, baby," I replied as our entrees arrived. There was the stuffed flounder for me and shrimp scampi for her. "I just need to get some more money together."

She sighed and shook her head. "So what does that mean? Another six months, another year, more trips to the hospital, more acupuncture for your shoulder?"

"No," I said. "It won't be that long."

"You said last night was going to be it."

"Hey, you always said the most important thing was that I came home," I replied.

"It is," she said. "But whether you come home or not isn't entirely up to you. Leaving our house, however, is. I don't want to be a widow at twenty-seven. Kayi can't grow up like this. I used to think that she could, but now I know she can't."

"She won't," I said sternly.

"Then tonight is it," she said after a sip of wine. "I know it's all of a sudden that I'm acting like this. But I've been thinking about it all day. You weren't even up to see us off this morning."

I pictured Adele in a cemetery, wearing a black dress with a veil over her face. My coffin was closed, and I saw her holding my little Kayi, tears streaming from behind her dark shades. That scene could have played out at any time. No real family man should have to carry a .380 in his coat for dinner with the wife.

"Tonight is it," I said as seriously as I knew how. "I promise."

We didn't talk much in the Acura on the way home. She drove and I stared out the window, watching the tunnel lights wash by as evening melted into night. Kayi was at my mother-in-law's and would be there until the morning. We could have had a night to ourselves, if I didn't have things to finish.

"You okay?" I asked her as we started up the walkway to the house. She seemed preoccupied with something out on the street.

114

"I'm alright," she said as she looked down the lawn. "I've just never seen those trucks before." She pointed to the two black Paths directly in front of our place. Something wasn't right. I reached under my coat for Mike's pistol.

"What are you doing?" she asked.

"Something's wrong," I said. "Take your car and go to your mama's. Don't call here and don't come back until you hear from me."

"What?" she asked confusedly. "Why?"

"Somebody's in the house," I whispered. Her eyes bulged. "And they ain't here to say hello."

"In the house? In *our* house?" she replied, whispering fearfully. She'd never been that close to it before. And I'd never wanted her to be. "How do you know? What . . . what are you gonna do?"

"Ask them to leave," I said, putting an index finger to my lips. My heart was already racing. She read my eyes and didn't say another word. Instead, she and her platform heels clopped back over to the driveway, where she started her engine and backed into the street. I watched her until she was out of sight.

I cocked my only weapon, longing for the Sigs that were still in their box in the basement. At the front door, I entered and turned my key harder than I usually would have. I wanted them to know that I was there. I turned the knob and pushed it open.

I jumped back onto the lawn as shotgun fire splintered the newly painted white door and the pine frame around it. They weren't aiming, just hoping that they'd hit something. The dogs a few yards over were barking like they were losing their minds.

I took those few seconds and entered the darkness of the foyer. I counted five figures as I emptied my tiny pistol toward where they stood. I scattered them, but no direct hits. It had to be the gun. I hated using other people's guns.

I darted through the living room while they got up from where they'd taken cover. I got to the kitchen just as buckshot shredded the dining room table. The blast was so close it grazed my right leg. The shit hurt like hell, but I kept it moving.

I flung the basement door open and galloped down the stairs. Halfway down I pulled down the hinged piece of Teflon I'd installed there and buckled it to the accompanying latch on the stairwell so that they couldn't follow. Ray thought I was a dumbass for spending the dough to get it installed. But I couldn't listen to a dude that worked for the post office.

The basement lights were already on. They'd ransacked the place in my absence, hoping to cut me off from my hardware before I could start putting holes in them. The finished bar was nothing but broken glass and spilled liquor. The leather couch had been ripped and sliced. The big-screen TV had been kicked in, and there were deep dents and gashes in the home theater. But they hadn't found my stash.

I kept all of the hardware in a compartment I built into the floor under the sofa. So I slid the ruined furniture aside, spun the combination dial in three different directions, and opened it up. I grabbed my Sigs, four clips, and two concussion grenades, the last of the crate I'd bought off this army munitions dude who had a gambling problem. I already had my vest on when I tucked the second pistol into my pants and flipped the first off safety.

Then I went into the laundry room, shut the door behind me, and opened up the safe, packing all the money I'd kept from Kamau's twenty grand into the backpack. That was when the basement windows started to shatter.

I smelled the gasoline before I saw it spilling down the wainscoted walls and onto the carpeted floor, mixing with the spilled alcohol that was already there. The only exit was just beyond the spreading pool of flammable liquid. I jumped over the stretching puddle and landed on the uncarpeted slab of concrete by the back exit.

Knowing that I didn't have much time, I took off the deadbolt and pushed the door. But it didn't budge. I looked out the window and saw that it was jammed by the pile of firewood that was left there from the previous winter. I turned back around to head for the stairwell only to see four tiny flames, most likely matches, coming through the broken window frames. I was trapped.

The flames rose. They engulfed the bar and slithered across the carpet toward the sofa. Even if I did manage to escape, my attackers would still be outside, waiting to see my face just so that they could shoot it off.

Quarts of sweat ran from every pore on my body. The thickening smoke started a coughing fit. I panicked. My visions of Adele as a widow were about to come true. They'd given me the absolute worst way to go. And there was nothing I could do about it.

Then it came to me. I pulled the pin on one of my two grenades and took as many steps back as I could. There were only seconds before I would start to suffocate. The blast nearly deafened me, even with my ears covered. I looked up and saw that the door had been hammered into pieces, most of which had been blown far out onto the lawn. I made my way past what was left, bag on my back and guns in each hand.

They'd left the backyard empty. I drew the second gun from the back of my pants and got ready to level the death squad that was probably waiting for me on the front lawn. But when I got there, it was deserted too. I stuffed both weapons into the back of my pants and covered them with my sweat-soaked blazer.

Neighbors had come from all around to look at the blaze

in wonder. I stopped to look too, frozen in disbelief that half of my home was covered in flames, cinders popping like it was a giant fire at a Boy Scout jamboree. Then that familiar echo of sirens entered my still painfully ringing ears. That was when Adele's Acura screeched to a halt in front of the burning residence we'd owned for almost a year.

She jumped out of her car and ran over to me. Then she froze too. You would've thought that we were looking at fireworks on the 4th of July. My Regal was on fire as well. Its tires had been slashed. Whether it was the gas furnace, the fuel tank in my car, or both, something was about to explode and take us with it. Plus, the cops would have questions I didn't want to answer, the kind of questions meant to ruin my squeaky-clean criminal record.

"Do you know where he is?" she asked. I nodded.

"I wanna see you do it," she said, more confident than I'd ever seen her. I nodded again, my eyes fixed on the white siding encasing our house as it slowly turned black. "I wanna see you put an end to this." I nodded again. Disbelief had my tongue in a chokehold.

"Then let's go!" she yelled. We tracked toward the Acura, which she bulleted down 10th like a crazy woman, heading for U Street. As we pulled off, I briefly saw the flashing lights pull up in front of our former residence. We'd gotten away just in time. The fire engine arrived first, which probably blocked the cops' view of our escape.

"You okay?" she asked me, her eyes glued to the road. "Did they hurt you?"

"Yeah, but I should be dead," I said.

"I had that .38 you gave me in the car," she said. Her hands were trembling. "I woulda killed 'em if you needed me to."

My stomach felt queasy, and my shoulder ignited again.

"I know you would've," I said. "I'm just glad you didn't have to."

"For better or for worse," she said. She still hadn't looked at me. And I didn't want to see what was behind her eyes, the cocktail of emotions that forced her face completely blank.

We had another house in Baltimore, one we'd bought for cheap at an auction a few months earlier. We had planned on renting it out. But if you ever want to make God laugh, then make plans.

"Where the fuck is he?" she asked.

"1949 Columbia Road, over by Trio's."

"And where we gonna go after that?" she asked, her tone switching to desperation.

"The house in B-more," I replied. "You remember where it is. If you don't, I'll drive—"

"No," she said coldly. "I'm gonna drive this fuckin' car. You're gonna let me have control of one goddamn thing tonight. And I'm gonna watch him die. You're gonna kill him right in front of me."

I didn't know what a nervous breakdown looked like or if there'd be divorce papers on the way to our future address. I didn't even know if I had the strength to pull another trigger. I'd just lost my home, my first home. But I had to be happy that it had stopped there. The family, all of us, were still intact.

It turned out that 1949 Columbia Road was a six-floor apartment building. Mike had once again given me just enough info to get him off the hook but not enough for me to know which of a hundred doors I needed to kick in. And Adele would make me kick in all of them. But God must have been looking out for me. Because Kamau walked right out of the front of the building with five beards in tow, probably the same five that had burned my house to a crisp.

"Is that them?" Adele asked.

"Yeah," I said. She still hadn't turned to look at me.

"I'm going to wait right here in the car. When you come back, I want this to be over with." That was my Adele. Everything had to be on her time.

"Alright," I said, already halfway out of the car.

She pulled off abruptly, and I stood there for a moment. I watched the group of men move closer and closer to the two black Pathfinders I saw parked a few cars down from where I stood. They were laughing and smiling, already drunk off of an unsealed victory. I was the last person they expected to see. They were just like all of the others. And there had been so many others.

I'd stood in that same place on a repeating loop for as long as I could remember. And now I was finally sick of doing the honors. But this one had to be done.

It was an exercise in marksmanship. I aimed for the head, through an eye, straight through a chest cavity. I was still a surgeon. I was going out on top.

Then four slugs unexpectedly rocked my own chest. Another pierced my thigh. I hit the pavement, barely knowing where I was. They'd all gotten shots off just before my bullets had made their mark.

I tried to get up, but my body wouldn't respond. The pain came from everywhere, and it was so blinding that I couldn't think. Then the coldness began, this icy feeling that crept up from my toes, through my legs, into my chest.

I saw all the things that had made up my life: drugs and death, so much blood, more slugs than I could count, too many men killed for nothing. Now I was going to join them. Live by the sword and all that. My weapons dropped to the asphalt from numb hands. It was almost over.

Then I saw my little baby as clear as day in the darkness behind my eyes. I saw the woman who had brought her into the world with me, and how they had been the only good things in my life for almost as long as I could remember.

I couldn't leave them in the world without me. I couldn't turn Kayi into another little girl who never knew her daddy. And with that the world came into focus and my eyes popped open as if they were seeing for the first time. The cold that was within me boiled over. And while I couldn't walk, I could crawl.

Turns out my enemies were all as dead as disconnected phones anyway, except for Kamau, who was on the ground with one in his abdomen. My aim was still deadly.

He crawled toward the jeeps, dragging a huge leather bag along with him. I crawled toward him, then planted my good leg under me and finally got to my feet. The wound in my thigh swelled with a rush of pain as I applied my weight to it, hobbling toward him, driven by nothing but the thought of the two people who brought me home every night.

Kamau moved like that serpent in the Garden of Eden, on his stomach. He really thought he had a chance of escaping. I hobbled in front of what was left of him and put the foot of my good leg against his spine, grinding his wound into the asphalt.

"Was it worth it?" I asked. I was in so much pain my eyes were tearing. A fatal wound must have been ten times worse.

"Yes," he hissed, struggling to get the words out. His breathing was shallow. "It was."

"It wasn't personal with Delante, you know?" I said.

He nodded. I was pretty certain that at least three of my ribs were broken.

I pulled the trigger for the last time in my life. The deepest red splattered onto the concrete beneath him and onto me, reminding me of Shaka all those years before. When I twisted around, Adele was at the curb with the engine running. I snatched the bag from the grip of Kamau's corpse and hobbled back toward my wife.

"You took too long," she said. I wanted to smile, but the loss of blood had weakened my sense of humor. I pulled back the zipper to see nothing but layers of green. We had our start-up money. I started to faint from loss of blood.

"Let's go," I said as my wife screeched off toward her mother's house to get the baby. I'd stop by Ray's to stitch myself up. And after that, we'd disappear forever.

Shaw and U Street would be flooded with badges looking for answers. Without a motive, the scene back at the house would make my family and me look like the victims. Any ballistics tests would come to a dead end when they couldn't find my guns. The fire would destroy any remaining evidence. Even tracing the Regal would lead them to a dead man named Nick Washington.

There was $750,000 in Kamau's bag. Added to my stash, we had the better part of a million.

I didn't know much about what lay ahead, only what was behind me. And like Spivy I was sure that I'd find myself up early, trying to do something that would overshadow the trail of death and tears I'd been paving for almost half of my life. I couldn't erase the past. I didn't think I could bury who I was and become something new. But at least I could try.

Epilogue

"Daddy?" she calls behind her for about the twenty-third time in the last three minutes. I am almost finished, my fat fingers struggling to make the tiny cornrows she always asks for. Her hair has gotten so long and thick since she was born that I have to do them diagonally and braid the ends into a kind of ponytail. Her mother taught me how to do this on a doll years ago, when we first moved in, back before she got sick, before the cancer had sucked her down to nothing in a matter of months, before the funeral where *he* cried for the first time in as long as *he* could remember.

"What is it honey?" I ask.

I didn't have to see her eyes just then to know that she was squinting them the way she did when she thought really hard about something. I knew because I did the same thing, because they had been my gift to her even if God and genetics had been the ones to put the package together seven years nine months and six days before. Her mama and I had been more than happy with the final product.

"Why did we leave DC when I was little?"

Why is it that kids always ask the questions grown folks don't want to answer? And why is it that the answers you want to give to your kids are ones they can never really understand until they're grown? It's one of those catch-22's that comes with parenthood. There has to be a method to the madness, a way to find balance between the truth and what makes sense, because the two are rarely the same.

"Your mother and I wanted a change," I say. "There was a lot of crime where we lived, and then our house burned down."

"Really?" she asks with surprise. "The whole house?"

"The whole house," I reply. "So we took the money from the insurance settlement and bought this place out here."

It was enough of the truth that it wouldn't sting so much years later when she was ready but still enough of a fantasy to protect her from who you used to be, from the psychopath who thought that what he was doing was okay as long as he only killed people who had killed other people. She asks you about the bullet scars all over you, and you say that you were in the Marines that fought in Iraq. That lie is one she spreads to anyone who'll ask. She's proud that her old man is a warrior. If she only knew how *much*.

So many bullets flew through the air, and the one that killed my baby didn't even come from a gun. Looking back, I know it was karma—except when it came back to me, she took the blow. She always said that she would.

I finish her hair, and she races up the two flights to her room to do her homework or watch TV or play with her PSP, whatever she does. Kids run everywhere, not because they're really in a rush but just because they can. At thirty-two, you try and do as few things as possible just because you can.

I sent Ray over to the house after the fire department put the blaze out. He said he had to go at like four in the morning so no one would notice him. The stairs weren't stable, and he almost fell through charred, brittle wood a couple of times. But he went and got a hold of all that was left—the hardware and some cash I'd tucked into a few places—and brought it all out. I offered him a few Gs for his trouble, but he wouldn't have it. He said his cut was just knowing that we were all okay. He and Thai are the only ones who know where I am, the only dudes with DC tags who ever get to ring my doorbell. Sometimes that's a good thing. Other times I wonder if home even exists anymore, if it was all in my mind in the first place.

At least I got my mama to move out this way. She told everybody it was because she got a house for real cheap and that the city wasn't the same since I moved away. I think she told most people Chicago, but you never can tell how long your mama's gonna keep a lie straight. There's a cop that sweeps by her place every now and again. I think he hopes to see me sitting in a rocking chair on her rowhouse stoop, like I'm gonna be out there waiting for him to bust me.

I didn't have to change my name, since hardly anyone knew it anyway. I'm sure there are warrants out, but I'm never getting close enough to Shaw for me to get served. And out here I'm a businessman, owner and operator of AK (Adele and Kayi's) Carwash on the West Side. We serve all kinds of people, and we do pretty okay. I still wanna add that other business in, but I haven't had the time. Being legit is the real fuckin' grind. Sitting at that desk and answering the phone. You're a slave to the time and place, even if you own it.

I still keep two Sigs in the basement with two clips. They're registered, but I haven't as much as touched them since we got here. That part of my life is over. That part of me died and became something else. Maybe it was more a father. Maybe it was me as widower instead of husband. Maybe it was just me being too old for all that shit. Either way, it drives me crazy sometimes, the quiet and the peace. It doesn't seem natural even when I know how much Kayi needs it to grow up to be the woman I want her to be.

* * *

It's a Saturday outside, maybe four in the afternoon. There's not a cloud in the sky except for the smoke coming from the Domino plant. Sounds like a day for seafood or Italian down at the Harbor. Or maybe we'll just go for a walk or hit the wax museum my little girl is so in love with for the twentieth time in the last six months. I am on my way up to her room to ask about it when the phone rings. On the other end is a voice I haven't heard in a little while.

"Snow, it's Thai."

"Wassup, main man?" I reply, smiling. "It's been a minute."

What comes back isn't excitement or celebration. It's all sad.

"It's Ray. He's gone."

"Gone where?" I ask, not allowing myself to get it. "What, he ran off with some broad or something?"

"He's dead. Somebody shot him. They found him floating in the Anacostia."

Something starts to burn inside of me, but I can't tell where it's coming from. I keep seeing him when he came out to watch the game just a few months before. Skins against the Giants, an old-ass grudge that started when we were still kids, back when bitch-ass Phil Simms went on TV talking about how he was going to Disney World. Fuck his cracka ass!

"What do you mean?" I ask, still not letting it sink in.

"I'm on my way to your house," Thai says. "I'll be there in less than an hour. Don't go nowhere."

"I won't," I say.

My first impulse is to grab my daughter and pack a bag for both of us and check into a hotel for the rest of the weekend. If I do that, Thai comes to an empty house and it's back to car washing come Monday morning when I'm due back. Things are simple now, and safe. No surprises. No threats. We're all grown men. This is something for the cops to handle.

But my soul can't even let those thoughts finish. No matter where I go, I'm a nigga from Shaw, and Ray and Thai and E were the ones who always had my back. Something tells me there was something inside, just below the surface of all our fallen homies, something that has to do with our past, something that started with Ray but is heading straight for us, something we can't run from. But we can go to war. That's what I do, after all.

Instead of going up to Kayi I go down to the basement. The Sigs are sealed in a metal box beneath the circuit breakers. The combination is Adele's birthday. As I get the steel in my palm, it feels like seven years has been a day. I feel like a killer again, and I can't tell yet if that's a good or a bad thing.

SNOW

KENJI JASPER

The following questions are intended to enhance
your group's discussion of
this book.

DISCUSSION QUESTIONS

1. How does fatherhood affect Snow? Does it make him complacent and "soft" or does it focus him and make him "harder"?

2. Is there anything Snow's mother could have done to keep him off the streets? What would have made a difference in his life? More money? A father? A different environment?

3. When Snow witnesses the robbery and killing of Mr. Seasons, what else could he have done differently? Why is Mr. Seasons so important to Snow that he would risk getting involved?

4. Why does Landy decide to shoot Charles rather than dealing with the issue some other way? How does that decision affect Snow's life?

5. How does Snow justify his actions? At what point does he cross the line from just "doing the right thing" and become a "menace to society"?

6. When Snow first reveals his line of work to Adele in the restaurant, she says "every job has its risks," like it doesn't bother her. Is this how she really feels at the time? Does her father's experience as a hustler affect the way she feels? Why does her opinion about Snow's work change later? How does motherhood affect her feelings?

7. When Snow kills the seventeen-year-old girl at the poker game, his only reaction is to say, "That was unfortunate." How does he reconcile his love for his wife and daughter with his calm detachment in committing crimes? Is he a psychopath? Or would you prefer to call him "professional"?

8. Why does Chandra put up with Shaka's abuse? After Snow rescues Chandra and gets beaten down for it, how does he feel about Chandra's devotion to Shaka? Does Snow rescue Chandra because he wants to help her or because he wants to get with her? When he later "cashes in his prize" and sleeps with her, does he like her less or more than when he first laid eyes on her?

9. What does Ray mean when he asks Snow, "You think you Jesus or somethin'?" When Snow replies that he just wants to do what's right, Ray tells him, "Around here, you wanna always do what's right for you." What does he mean by this?

10. How does getting arrested affect Snow's worldview? Why doesn't he go straight?

11. When Snow's mother learns of his misdeeds, he seems to be genuinely upset. And while his friends try to tell their parents that they are not so bad, Snow does nothing of the sort. "I knew better," he says to himself. "And I respected Ma too much to try to play her for a fool. We both knew that I was bad. And I wasn't sure if I'd ever be good again." Is Snow really so bad, compared to his friends? Isn't he holding himself to a

much higher standard than most of the young men he knows?

12. Is Kamau the villain of the book? Is Snow the hero? What do these labels have to do with the real world depicted in the novel?

13. In the epilogue, what does Snow mean when he says that his wife's cancer was karma? What did she do to deserve an early death?

14. What does Snow mean when he says he doesn't know if it's a good thing or a bad thing that he feels like a killer? What do you think? Is it good or bad?

The following excerpt is from
C-Murder's powerful debut novel
DEATH AROUND THE CORNER,
another VIBE Street Lit title
available now from Kensington.

"Macy! Macy! Can we go to the fair?"

"Daquan, for the last time, I'll take you to the fair! Now shut the hell up, boy!"

Daquan stared at the TV screen, wide-eyed with excitement and anticipation after hearing his mother's confirmation. Never mind her tone or the fact that his last birthday he never got the Big Wheel she promised, still she was Mommy and her words filled him with happiness.

The World's Fair of '84 was the biggest thing he had seen in his life. The commercial showed all the happy faces, shiny gadgets, fun rides, and delicious food; things he'd never experienced in his five-year-old world. All he knew was the Magnolia Projects. One of the roughest, most drug-infested housing projects in New Orleans, Magnolia was a world in and of itself. Despite its squalid conditions, there were plenty of other kids and large grassy areas to play every game imaginable. The surrounding recreational parks had basketball hoops for the older cats, but at his age, Thomas Lafont Elementary was Daquan's very own amusement park, complete with monkey bars and seesaws and located right in the heart of the 'Nolia. Many a day he had gotten his ass torn up for going to Lafont without Macy's permission. Daquan wasn't a bad child, just a poor one, which meant he had to make do with whatever he had. And when it came to fun, Lafont was all he had. But now that the World's Fair was coming, it was like an early Christmas, and Daquan couldn't wait.

"Yeah, yeah," he squealed like a mini–Lil' Jon. "I'm goin' to the fair!"

He hopped down off of the clean but worn-down plastic-covered couch and crossed the living room, entering the kitchen. "I hope my daddy can come with us," he said to himself as he opened the refrigerator, looking for Kool-Aid. "He works too much," he added as an afterthought.

His father, Daryl, worked at Gambino's Bakery, sometimes working a double shift just to make ends meet and keep the bills paid in their one-bedroom apartment. He wouldn't let Macy work because he was raised knowing it was the man's responsibility to provide for his family. But in the era of Reaganomics, it was becoming next to impossible to do that alone. Still, he did the best he could, and Daquan loved him for it.

Daquan balanced the half-full pitcher of Kool-Aid between his chin and hands as he carried it to the table. He looked in the refrigerator and could basically figure out what his next meal would be. Inside was leftover red beans and rice, a hard block of commodity cheese, a box of corn flakes, and a box of powdered milk, so he knew it would be red beans and rice, unless his daddy brought home some eggs so Macy could make his favorite, scrambled eggs and rice.

He looked around for a clean glass or a mayo jar to drink from, but he couldn't find one. He ran to his parents' bedroom door and yelled, "Macy! I need a glass."

"Boy, if you don't get away from my damn door!"

Daquan stepped back from the door. He knew she wasn't in there alone. He knew Teddy, his father's cousin, was in there, like he was almost every day at this time. He often wondered what they did in there. But since Teddy and Daryl weren't only cousins, they were also friends, Daquan didn't see it as wrong in his five-year-old mind. He forgot about the Kool-Aid and walked away from the door, ready to take a nap and dream about the upcoming fair.

Inside the bedroom, Teddy remained jittery since Daquan had come to the door.

"Macy, you know I don't like coming to your house bringing you this stuff," he told her, sliding his works into his small leather pouch.

He was a petty hustler, homely looking and stupid, but Macy depended on him to keep the monkey off her back. As her habit grew, it got harder and harder to hide from Daryl that she was getting high again. Besides, money was tight, and right about now the only thing tighter was her pussy, which she had recently started offering Teddy in return for the dope.

"Teddy, stop bitchin'! The boy don't know nothin'. He ain't but five," she replied, feeling the china white slowly coat her mind with that serene nothingness. "I'm feelin' good, and this clown blowin' my high," she thought, eyelids at half-staff.

Still worried, he asked, "Why can't we meet somewhere else? Shit, Daquan might say the wrong thing. Man, look . . ." His voice trailed off.

Macy knew how to shut him up. She began to undress, revealing a petite but curvaceous frame. She watched Teddy's eyes fill with lust at her chocolate femininity.

"Daryl don't get home till eight, and it ain't but four," she said. "Now, do you want some pussy or not? 'Cause I know a lot of nigguhs who would love to be in your shoes."

Teddy watched her slowly massage her face and breasts, something she did routinely after getting hit with her fix, and it never failed to turn him on. She lay back on the bed and spread her long, dark legs invitingly. She was feeling good, and she wanted to pay Teddy before her high went down and the reality of her betrayal came raining down on her.

At the sight of her naked wetness, Teddy's heart began to beat a rhythm through his erection. He knew this was wrong. She was Daryl's wife. Daryl was his cousin. But he had never had a woman so beautiful, and if it wasn't for her addiction, he never would again.

"You are beautiful, baby, I just can't get enough of you," he whispered as he mounted Macy and entered her. "Girl, you got some good pussy. This the best I done had yet . . . How come you never let me kiss them pretty lips or change positions?"

She eyed him coldly. "Just fuck me, and when you cum, don't make a lot of noise. My baby in the other room."

Her mind wandered away from the man on top of her to the man she had betrayed. The guilt of knowing how much Daryl loved her made her hate herself for being so weak. Hating her need for the drug that had taken so much from her and always threatened to take more. At her lowest moments, she contemplated suicide. The thought of taking her own life had begun eight years ago, after losing her daughter, Diana, at birth. Macy knew it was because of her heroin use during pregnancy, and she had vowed to Daryl and herself that she'd stay clean—a promise she couldn't keep. Whenever Macy got high and thought of Diana, the tears would flow constantly and uncontrollably, like clockwork.

"Girl, why you always cryin' while we fuckin'?" Teddy asked between humps but received no answer. "Ain't it good to you, baby?"

His words fell on deaf ears because Macy was in her own

world. A world where happiness will never come, where she convicted herself as a murderer of her own flesh and blood and betrayed her only love.

Her thoughts were suddenly interrupted by a slight noise coming from the living room. "Was that the door?" she asked herself, quickly glancing at the clock. She held her breath, listening intently, until she mentally dismissed the sound as either the TV or Daquan.

Daryl looked at the stitches in his hand and chuckled to himself lightly as he got off the bus in front of the 'Nolia.

"Hell of a way to get the day off," he said to himself.

He had been at work washing dishes when he accidentally cut his hand on a knife.

The cut wasn't serious, but it did require stitches. He was sent to Charity Hospital and given the rest of the day off. A little family time was a welcome idea, being that he worked so hard.

Every morning he was up at four in order to make the two-hour bus ride to Metairie, some thirty miles west of New Orleans, where Gambino's Bakery was located. In a car, it would only take thirty minutes, but that was a luxury Daryl could not afford.

Regardless, he wasn't fazed or frustrated by his current situation, because at age twenty-five, he already had a plan. He wanted to own his own bakery one day, then build and expand. He already knew the proper functioning of the business, so he told himself that with hard work and patience, he would achieve his dream.

Daryl grew up hard. He had even done three years as a juvenile at Scotland Correctional Institute in eastern Louisiana. But he vowed to himself that he'd get his family out of the 'Nolia and into a better quality of life. Daryl had already seen what ghetto life had done to his young wife, but he stuck by her in hopes that love could conquer all.

He slid his hand into his pocket and winced from the pain of the still-tender cut, not yet knowing that it was nothing compared to the pain he'd soon face inside his own home. He opened the door, entered, and then quietly closed it behind him. This was the sound Macy heard that put her senses on alert. Cartoons played quietly on the TV as Daquan lay on the couch in a peaceful sleep. Daryl sat down next to Daquan and gently kissed his slumbering son on the forehead. He admired his features, focusing on the thick eyebrows they both had. But he had Macy's nose and a mixture of his caramel complexion and Macy's Hershey hue.

His contemplative mood was suddenly interrupted by noises coming from the bedroom. There was a thud, and his instincts intensified his hearing, turning the noises into a man's voice and then the unthinkable . . .

The sexual sounds of a man being pleased.

Before his mind had fully grasped the situation, his body reacted and took the initiative to rush the door.

Locked.

With all of his six-foot, two-hundred-twenty-pound frame, he coiled his leg and aimed for the right side of the doorknob, kicking the flimsy door off of its top hinge. He didn't want to believe his eyes. He *wished* he didn't have to believe what he saw, but what he saw could not be denied. Teddy leaped from between Macy's legs and stared at Daryl with total fear in his eyes.

"D-Daryl, man, look," Teddy stuttered. But all Daryl could say was, "I got cut." The rage inside was building like a runaway locomotive.

"You fuckin' bitch, I got cut," he screamed at his wife,

who was the only one who knew the full significance of the statement.

Macy was frantic, screaming apologies while Teddy tried to cover his shamed nakedness.

"You dirty bitch, I bled for you," Daryl hissed.

Macy looked into her husband's eyes and saw a look she'd never seen before. It was like only a shell was there, his soul totally void. He moved in a zombielike state as he turned his gaze to the doorless closet space a few feet away. Macy saw him, sensed his intentions, and yelled, "No, no, no, Daryl . . . I'm sorry . . . I swear I'm sorry!" But it was too late.

Daryl dug through the piled-up clothes and found the shoebox containing the .38 his father had given him. In an instant, the gun was in his hand. Teddy had no room to get out, so when he saw the gun, all he could do was back into the corner.

"Daryl, I swear to God, man, please just listen," Teddy pleaded. But Daryl's heart couldn't be reached, nor could his mind comprehend.

Teddy released his bowels as Daryl pointed the gun at him then, without hesitation, began to fire . . . and fire . . . and fire, until the revolver was spent and Teddy's chest was riddled. His body violently jerked as each hollow tip impacted with his chest and stomach. Teddy's torso seemed to inflate to twice its size, like a balloon filling with air, then quickly deflated to normal size. His body slid down the wall, lifeless, staring at nothing.

Daryl was snapped out of his trance by Macy's screams and Daquan's crying. His son had witnessed it all from the doorway.

"Daddy, please stop! Please, I'm scared."

At the sound of his son's voice, Daryl dropped the gun and turned to the crying boy.

"Come here, Daddy," Daquan sobbed. "Pick me up."

Daryl picked up Daquan, cradling him in his arms, and walked into the living room. Never once did he look at Macy or acknowledge her whimpers.

"Daryl," she kept repeating. "Daryl, I'm sorry."

He sat on the couch with Daquan on his lap. He knew he was on borrowed time.

There would be no running for Daryl. No hiding. He was a man raised to be a man and had done nothing any man in his position wouldn't do. Now all that was left were these last few words he had for his son, from the deepness of his heart.

"Baby boy, you know your daddy loves you with all his heart. I'm sorry about everything you saw. Daddy didn't mean to scare you. I love you. Don't ever forget that, okay?"

They were both crying now. Daquan's tears were the tears of a child losing his world and Daryl's the tears of a man being destroyed.

"I love you too, Daddy," Daquan answered.

"Now, they're gonna take me away for a long time, so I need you to be a little man and do the right thing."

"Nooo, Daddy! We can go away. We can run."

Daryl silenced his son. "No, a man *never* runs, you hear me? A man never runs."

These were words Daquan would never forget. Daryl hugged his son tightly and continued, making the most of the little time they had left. "I'll always be here for you. I'll write you letters and talk to you on the phone. You can even come see me, okay?"

It seemed to Daquan's young mind that the police were kicking in the door the very next moment. They rushed in, slamming his father to the ground.

"Get off my daddy!" Daquan yelled with all the manliness he could muster.

"Calm down, Daquan, I'm okay," Daryl assured him, facedown on the floor.

But it wasn't okay to Daquan.

Macy, shameful and shaken, called Daryl's mother to come get Daquan. He would never see Macy again. He sat alone outside amongst throngs of nosy neighbors and flashing police lights. All he could think about was how the cops took his daddy away, and a new emotion sprung into his young heart.

Hate.

It was making him see everything in a different light.

Please visit www.deatharoundthecorner.com *for more information.*